SEPTEMBER 2024 - ISSUE 216

# FICTION

# NON-FICTION

Neil Clarke: Publisher/Editor-in-Chief
Sean Wallace: Editor
Kate Baker: Non-Fiction Editor/Podcast Director

Clarkesworld Magazine (ISSN: 1937-7843) • Issue 216 • September 2024

© Clarkesworld Magazine, 2024.
clarkesworldmagazine.com

# The Music Must Always Play
## MARISSA LINGEN

The aliens took a large part of Mankato, Minnesota, with them when they went. Their ship was a little under five kilometers in diameter, which wiped out about a third of the center of Mankato when it crashed, but there was the debris field to think of. The Minnesota River Valley had dealt with tornados, it had seen dozens of floods, but this was beyond its experience—or anyone else's. Disaster relief teams came down from the Twin Cities, with frantic scientists close at their heels: the balance of saving lives and preserving evidence of an alien culture was not obvious to anyone, and it seesawed alarmingly in the days after the ship came down.

The whole world held its breath when a door opened and a bipedal figure staggered out—orangish, small, gesticulating with clear intent to communicate. Oozing red from the head, which the disaster relief workers and the scientists swiftly could agree was probably blood or its equivalent, probably important. They sprang into action, isolation suits covering all, a quarantine zone starting at St. Peter twenty-five kilometers away.

There were two living aliens left when the ship crashed Three days later, despite the best efforts of the Mayo Clinic and the National Guard, there were none. The breathless world clung to its loved ones and wept for a species it had never gotten to know.

The President of the US and the Secretary-General of the UN gave somber, appropriate speeches, commending the dead to whatever haven awaited orange aliens, praising their sacrifice and speaking of a future time when they would arrive intact. One of the four surviving faculty members at Minnesota State University-Mankato was shoved in front of cameras, glassy-eyed and dazed, to make comforting remarks to the rest of the world, which was not a notable success. And then the scientists and disaster relief crews could get down to work.

Maryam Mohamed had dreamed of, but not expected, a first contact in her lifetime—certainly not one within a few hours' drive of home. Her imagined version would have involved surviving aliens, a way to use her linguistics training slowly, painstakingly, to create understanding. Instead she found herself with the equivalent of an engraved mountain, covered inside and out with characters—symbols? pictures?—she had no native speaker to illuminate for her. She was assigned to the written portion of the language, which involved spending most of her days examining and recording the inside of the gigantic spaceship. She didn't wear jilbab like some of her cousins, which was a relief, because the options for isolation suits were still not optimized for them.

She spent the first week walking around the ship making notes to herself about what might be useful to study closely, what could confirm assumptions from previous areas, what was too contaminated with the corpses of their visitors and the detritus of their deaths. The constant background whistling and thumping was distracting at first, but soon it resolved into melodies, rhythms. She knew that there were others assigned to parsing it as either language or art, and she could let it fade into her own background, like having alien radio all the time, though of course it could be disaster announcements or the equivalent of a podcast or—anything really. She knew it was anthropomorphizing to ascribe melancholy to the alien ship's constant sounds, but there it was all the same.

When she finally stumbled upon another isolation-suited figure—she could go all day without seeing anyone—there was finally someone to hear some of those feelings. "They came so close," she said wistfully.

The person turned, and Maryam realized it was Sean Thao, a biologist she'd met during their brief, harried site orientation. "Maybe not that close. If they'd lost most of the crew partway through the trip, their decay rates may have been slowed in this controlled environment."

"But if they'd been losing people gradually for years, they'd have had a chance to clean up the bodies."

He winced. "Good point. Hope our containment suits are as good as they say."

"Hope our biologies are incompatible," she returned. The minute it was out of her mouth she was afraid she had alienated someone she'd have to work with for months, but his sympathetic grimace said that he had already thought of that.

That night her father was restless on video chat, a sign of a bad pain day. Maryam struggled to think how to frame her day to hold his interest when the cancer treatment—and wrangling the disintegrating medical system to get it—consumed his focus. "Lots of progress today, Aabe!" she chirped cheerfully, editing out the bodily fluids, the corpses. "I really think I've got a handle on how to organize this work."

He forced a brief, exhausted smile. "You were always the organized one, maandheey. Your sister and I are managing without you, but . . . "

Zeinab's face appeared in the background, still visibly rolling her eyes. "We're *fine*, don't worry. I've even gotten the paperwork done for our application for in-home nursing assistance, so I don't know why *you're* getting credit for being the organized one. Aabe's just having a tough day with the nausea, that's all."

So Maryam wasn't the only one trying to edit the bodily fluids out of the conversation. She made a sympathetic face. "I know Zeinab's got you hooked up with the lemon ice, though," she said encouragingly. The rest of the conversation focused entirely on her father's struggles, and it ended sooner than she had expected, with no further word about the epoch-making work she was doing.

Her father had been frustrated when she chose linguistics as a career—and entirely boggled when she got a job with benefits doing it. Like many immigrants, he had hoped that a career in medicine or engineering would see his children safely through their adult lives with a solid salary and health care. He had understood and cheered Zeinab's choice of civil engineering. Maryam's progression to the heady heights of linguistics research had started with gradual, grudging acceptance, moving only slowly into baffled respect as she racked up accolades.

And now there was this: the decision to go into the quarantine zone, to head south to the ruins of Mankato and let Zeinab bear his time in chemo for both of them. He had told her to go, seeing clearly that the opportunity would define her career, even have global implications. Zeinab had practically packed her bag for her. But that didn't mean it was easy to watch her father's decline through a screen, so close and unable to make the drive—hardly more than an hour—to hug him.

If she'd gone into medicine she might have been able to help. But she had never really considered it, never wanted to do anything but linguistics—until now, when he needed her. Even with her mother's death, she had not really imagined that her father could also die.

She wondered if there was someone back on a distant planet thinking the same about every single individual on the ship she spent her days examining.

After hanging up the call, she reviewed her notes from the day, trying to redirect her thoughts to a more cheerful topic—or at least one she could do something about. She glanced around her temporary apartment, noticing writing everywhere she looked—not just her books and laptop keyboard but the brand names of the appliances, the function buttons that set the oven to broil or bake, even light switches labeled with their off and on positions. And she was going to have to figure out which words meant off and on and which meant Manufactured By the Alien Space Corporation and which meant Blessed by the Alien Space Religion—and which ones weren't words at all, they were just ornamental squiggles.

She was going on the assumption that the giant ship was only using one language, as a simplifying first thought, but even in the rental apartment, her own household had five languages printed on things she'd bought and brought in: English, of course, and Spanish and French depending on whether the company intended to sell the same product in Mexico or Canada, and then a few toiletries and spices of her own with printing in Somali and Arabic. How could she assume that an entire ship full of thousands of aliens would be simpler than her own life? But how could she make any progress any other way? Maryam didn't sleep well, her dreams echoing with whistles and thumps. The next day was another flood of data taking, another avalanche of hopeful fellow creatures dead where they had stood.

As the weeks went by, the biology team and the cleanup crew made enough progress that Maryam was no longer finding dead aliens every shift, which was a relief. She didn't want to ever grow that accustomed to death, and though they were clearly not human, they were equally clearly sentients, trying desperately to go about the business of life.

The other major relief was that no adverse effects were reported in the quarantine zone. Sprained ankles and high blood pressure showed up at the same rates as always, and anxiety was slightly elevated, but so far, at least, there was no sign of radiation sickness, no alien virus, no cloud of fungus infesting the lungs of those in the crash zone, which was now euphemistically being called the landing zone. It didn't mean that she could visit someone as fragile as her father right away—but it gave her hope that this separation wouldn't be forever. More importantly, that it wouldn't be the rest of his life.

And, of course, that there would be no worldwide alien plague that wiped out life as she had previously known it. The world, the fate of humanity, felt like it *should* be more important—but her mind kept circling back to her father and her sister, struggling through Aabe's chemo together without her. She could make herself focus on work— work was full of fascinating challenges—but everything that was not work was a vague blur, impossible to focus on when there was the course of her father's treatment to think of.

The other scientists were restless for their own reasons, and at first Maryam was too wrapped up in her own work and family life to care much what they were. There wasn't much to do in the temporary housing, and the ad hoc book swaps and movie nights made less and less difference as the novelty of the situation wore off. She spent barely enough time with the others at meals to notice that something was off, but she couldn't let it be her problem.

That lasted until she made a breakthrough on a piece of writing present throughout the ship: she leaned against a panel in frustration and the ship soundtrack audibly changed for the whole time she was leaning, the thumps growing faster and louder. Was it a coincidence? She stood up and it was restored to normal.

She found another example of the writing and leaned on it, and the thumps grew faster and louder again. "Yessssss," she said. She wrote up notes on this and went to the cafeteria, looking for someone to chatter to about it. Sean Thao was there eating a sandwich and looking morose, so she spilled the day's triumphs out to him.

"Does it mean 'next track'? 'start emergency communication'? '*stop* emergency communication'? 'I'm about to input something important, pay attention'? 'By the grace of our gods or our rulers do the dance that goes with this song'? I don't know," Maryam babbled. "But now we know that pressing the thing that looks like *this* changes the sounds. And that's the first thing we can say for sure. That's the first piece."

"Great, amazing," said Sean, but his scowl said the opposite.

"What's wrong with you?"

"Nothing, I'm just—it seems like such a small thing, with everything that's going on in the world."

Maryam scrunched up her nose. "What are you talking about?"

"Haven't you been following the news?"

"We *are* the news."

She had meant that to be a joke, but Sean huffed in exasperation. "There have been riots. At least a hundred killed just today."

"Where?" She blinked and tried again for coherence: "*Why?*"

He grimaced. "Everywhere. Because of this. Because of them."

She shook her head, uncomprehending.

"We wondered if we were alone in the universe. And now the answer is—what? No? Maybe yes, now? Who knows? And people—are not handling it well. Politicians, normal people, no one is handling it well."

"Obviously we're not alone," Maryam murmured.

"What if they were the last survivors of their planet? What if we were only not alone for those three days, while they were gasping and dying?"

Maryam lost patience. "Well, what if! What if there are millions of other planets full of intelligent life and they're all dying, all of them, this very moment, what if your mother and your brother and your whole family are all in a plane crash right now and you don't know you're alone yet, what if the alien ship knocked a bunch of meteors loose and they're all headed for us, what if we've already inhaled whatever killed them and we'll fall over at the next cookout we go to, the next graduation party, the next wedding. What if. What does that change *now*."

"Everything," Sean sputtered. "How can it not change everything."

"Tell me one everything."

He stared at her.

"I'm being serious. If it changes everything, it shouldn't be hard to point at one everything."

"If you know you're about to lose someone—"

"I do know that."

The quality of his silence shifted abruptly. "Maryam, I'm sorry, I had no idea."

She shrugged impatiently. "We're work friends. Why would I bring it up."

Sean squirmed. She could watch him trying to figure out how to ask who it was, who she expected to lose, without being even more horrifically insensitive. Finally she gave in. "My dad is going through chemo right now. My sister is handling his care."

"And you're—"

"I'm here trying to do science, Sean." He looked overwhelmed, so she went on. "So yeah. It's worthwhile to keep trying to figure things out. Yeah, it's worthwhile to be here. Is it the only worthwhile thing, no, obviously not. But—you only get the days you get, and you don't get to know how many days. My mom died years ago. Car accident. Nobody could have seen it coming. And it mattered that she was with us, even though she's gone. And it will matter that my dad has been with us, even when he goes. And it matters, of course it matters, that these aliens—these *people*—came to see us. Even if they didn't make it. And you're telling me people are *killing* each other over this? Over *this*?"

He was silent for a moment, and she decided to just sit with the silence, to let him think about it. "The riots are," he hesitated. "They're not really *at* anybody. They just . . . get out of hand."

"Humanity," she said, pronouncing it like a curse. "Getting out of *hand*. Over someone coming to visit."

Sean looked at his hands. "I don't know, obviously I don't condone rioting, but—I can see why people are messed up about this. I get them.

But I didn't think about it your way, I just—it's really disappointing, you know?"

Maryam did know. She had not let herself feel the disappointment—it felt ungrateful, being handed a treasure trove of alien language and complaining that it had not arrived in her exact preferred form. She had allowed—forced, really—tunnel vision, because anything more was overwhelming. But she had to admit that when she let herself think about all the dead aliens as potential research collaborators, neighbors, *friends*, it was all rather grim.

Unfortunately she couldn't see a way to translate an alien message of hope even if there was such a thing upon the ship—not any time soon, not soon enough to reach the panicking, rioting peoples of Earth. She was thrilled to have gotten to the point where she could recognize one inscription that changed ship sounds—that was miles from knowing how to say, "don't give up," or "we come in peace." Light years, really.

Deep into the night, Maryam looked at her laptop as if it would provide any kind of answer. Of course it was not the site of storage for the vast majority of the photographic evidence she had of the alien writing and potential writing—only the images she was most immediately working on. But it suddenly felt heavy laden, stuffed full.

She knew what she needed to do.

The site directors were not initially receptive to her idea of releasing a livestream not of images but of sound from the crashed ship. None of them were fans of the live elephant, polar bear, and panda cams that had populated the internet for decades, so they didn't immediately see what a ship feed would do. But Maryam was persistent and enlisted surprised members of the music linguistics team to help her argue, and the feed went live despite official misgivings.

It was only a week later—a week with no breakthroughs in her own work, a week of grind and frustration—that Zeinab sent her a link to a remix with the alien sounds in it. "I played this for Aabe so he'd know what you were working with," her text read. "He smiled and even grooved a little." The remix had millions of views and comments.

Maryam was aware of smiling so hard her cheeks hurt. She was only belatedly aware of tears running down her face.

She made herself look at the news sites then, only then, and it looked like the riots were easing as people came to terms with the crash. As people thought about the aliens the way she had—lost collaborators, lost partners—they let themselves grieve, and some people's grief was turning to art. It was the best she could do for everyone else.

It was time to do the next thing for herself.

The alien language project would probably take the rest of her career and beyond. They'd had months to monitor, and no one working on the project had an alien disease that anyone could detect. She could take some time without it being a permanent surrender. She would be the first of the scientists to go into a few weeks of solo quarantine and back into the outside world, her own long journey that she hoped would bring connection—as she could now see that the aliens had managed despite their untimely deaths. Making her father smile from a distance was all very well, but she had to hug him again, to see for herself how he was doing.

She was surprised at how supportive her colleagues were—except Sean, who knew the whole story. His support didn't surprise her a bit. "They'll miss you on the written language team," he said. "We all will. I will."

Maryam made herself paste on a smile. "I'll be back, though. There'll be plenty left to do when my leave is over. This isn't a project for an intern to knock out in one summer."

He barked out a laugh. "Don't we just wish. Figuring out how to communicate with another species, what kind of idiot could take more than a week to do that?" Then he turned serious again. "I hope your dad's doing okay. I hope the chemo works."

"Me too. Thanks."

"Hey, maybe . . . maybe another ship will come. Maybe we'll figure out some of their language and the next batch of them will make it to actually *talk* to us."

"Yeah, maybe. But for now we know they were out there, and that's got to be enough. And we can groove with them. I'll send you the link. It's . . . maybe it'll give you a little more hope about people. Human people, not just the new ones."

He smiled. "I'd like that."

## ABOUT THE AUTHOR

**Marissa Lingen** writes fantasy, science fiction, poetry, and essays. She lives in the Minnesota River Valley near its confluence with the Mississippi and is cheerfully obsessed with its geology and limnology. She is also inordinately fond of trees, tisanes, dark chocolate, and Moomins.

# Fish Fear Me, You Need Me
## TIFFANY XUE

Mac comes in after running around the little island we live on—used to be ten laps, then it became twenty, now thirty—all sweaty and out of breath and says, "Good weather for fishing today."

I nod because at this point and with his predilections, he's always the final vote on whether or not we fish. It's like my Ma used to say, "Happy wife, happy life", except I've never been married, and Mac's wife went underwater twenty-three years ago. He and I met six months after that, him in a little sad raft surviving off of cans of sardines packed before the floods and the fish, and me in my little apartment in the house on my used-to-be-big island. He was tan and burnt from sun exposure, his hair bleached and tacky because he thought dunking his head underwater was enough to keep it clean and keep himself cool.

"Where'd you come from?" was the first thing I said to him, shotgun pointed at his groin—if he was a threat, I'd outthreat him.

"Springfield." He coughed and paused. "Western Mass." As if he would've survived from any other Springfield.

"Springfield's underwater."

"Why'd you think I'm here? Not for your ugly ass." Another cough. He hadn't had water in who knows how long. I got all mine from the sky at that point, would be another year before I got a better filtering system up and running.

"Trying to raid."

"For what? I've got no home, you fucker."

What could I do? I helped him off the boat, got him some water, and gave him my bed. I should have kicked him out like the stray dog he was, but I never had the heart to. Now, once a week, when it's not too sunny and the tide is high, Mac and I go fishing on the Charles, or at least where it used to be. Nostalgia and old habits, I guess. We go where there's a bit of salt in the air, and we go on those days because there's more fish when the water's high, more layers for them to be hiding in, and because Mac can't take the sun. I always bring my shades, but he always forgets, and he can't handle the glare of the water. I offer mine every time, but he always says no, and I'm glad because I don't think I could handle the glare either—that's why I have the shades—and secretly I'm pissed because he could just take the damn glasses and spare us the martyrdom.

I watch Mac, who's sponging off with a sweat rag hung up by the door. He could go for a swim, it'd be easier, but he never does.

"After breakfast?" I ask. He nods and goes to get some smoked gull, but stops, and stares into the smokebox for a moment.

"There's just one piece left," he says.

"I haven't been taking any," I say before he has a chance to accuse me of anything. I know Mac likes eating birds more than fish, even though there are fewer and fewer birds every day and the fish are only ever multiplying. Sometimes Mac would try to starve for a day or two before caving and eating some of what I got. I don't like it when he tries to starve himself like that.

"We got a gull just last week," Mac says, as if that'll put some food in the smokebox.

"That was two weeks ago. And it was a skinny bastard, that thing." Nearly snapped a herring off my line and took my finger with it. I grabbed it by the neck before it could get away and snapped the spine, still surprised that I had that in me.

"Did you eat its bits yet?" Mac asks.

"When have you ever wanted to eat those?"

"I dunno. You always take them with your fish when we've got gonads. Maybe they're good."

"They're *mine*. Medicine, Mac. Agreement was I get the testes and you could get everything else. Half the time I get nothing and you get ovaries. How's that fair?"

"I don't want ovaries. You're the one who decided that."

"Then hurry up and eat the rest of your gull. I'm not waiting long for you."

Mac stares into the smokebox like a sad, dejected dog. Like he's seeing his wife. I sigh.

"We'll find another gull today, and if it's a boy, I'll even give you the balls. Or maybe we'll fish up a turtle, find some clams for you."

"I don't want those either," Mac murmurs.

"Just eat something already."

He looks around all sad-like, but he's always sad on fishing days. He likes fishing, I can tell, but that might just be because there's never anything else to do. No electricity, few books, little space, there's not much that can be done. Mac used to be a home inspector, traveling all over the tri-state area and looking for all the things that could go wrong and be done right. He used to be a car guy, driving a vintage sports car on the days he wasn't driving the work truck. Now, they're all underwater. Now, he only has an island.

And me.

I eat my haddock. Mac sneaks a fruit off the dying lime tree and eats it rind and all, and I pretend not to notice him.

We set off at nearly noon, later than I'd like but fine considering the clouds still haven't parted. Mac remembers his shades this time, but not his hat. I don't bother to remind him—he's gotta learn somehow.

We go north until we sail past the tops of the luxury buildings, the deck furniture either washed away by waves or, for the ones bolted down on the roof, bleached and brittled by sunlight. For a while, Mac and I wondered if those buildings had been raided, but we've never seen another soul around here and I've never heard of another soul in the world these past decades, so after a while, we stopped wondering that.

The rusted beams of the Hancock tower pass by and we stop seeing the tops of buildings and the shady hints of roads. Ahead of us, there's the remains of the skyline of Cambridge, the sign that we've gone far enough.

"Here," I say. Mac pulls down the sail and we wobble on the weak waves as we get our poles set up. We've got five thousand feet of line between the two of us. Years back I finally got into the jammed closet on the third-floor apartment and found a bunch of nylon thread for whatever sewing projects that tenant had going on. I braided them, spooled them up, and surprised Mac with them on his arrival anniversary. I don't know why I did that. We'll have enough to last us a hundred years. I doubt we've got twenty left.

We drop our lines at the same time, aiming for the deeps of the Charles. There's no big fish down there, not a lot of meat on the bones, but that's where everyone went after the floods. Mac thinks it's because they're ashamed of what they are now, but I just think they like the dark. He says I'm an asshole because I think I'm smarter than him. He always says that just because I was in the middle of a grad degree when the flood came. I'm not smart, though. I was repeating a class, fucking up my projects, doing work for genius professors who wouldn't give me the time of day but needed someone to do their chores. I'm not smart. I just happen to know that animals can't feel shame, no matter what they used to be.

Lines down, Mac and I sit back. We've got a cooler of half-briny water for the fish, two gallons of drinking water, a can of old instant coffee, salmon jerky, and I made sure to mix some salt, flour, and a bit of herbs from the garden together and fry them up into flour patties for Mac. I don't like it when he starves, no matter how hard it is on me for him to not starve. If he wants to be out here all day, I want him to not have to head back for something as stupid as a stomachache.

Mac splits his time between watching the sky, net in hand, and watching our poles. I split my time between watching my pole and watching Mac when he looks away. He's older than when we met, which is obvious, but sometimes I'm still surprised by that. You think you know how someone looks, through all his bad haircuts, hooks through the cheek, his laughter at my shitty jokes, his tears when he starves, drinks, remembers, and through every day of being the only person you ever see, but then one day you see him again and he's completely different. I wonder if he thinks the same thing when he sees me. I wasn't a pretty thing to look at before, and I'm certainly not now. I've caught glances in the mirror and the water; gray hair, shitty beard, chipped glasses, and sunspots on my ears. My cheeks are sagging and my neck is old. I don't hate it though; I look more masculine with age.

Mac chews on the inside of his cheek.

"Think it'll be today?" I ask, something thoughtful disguising something cruel disguising something selfish. I can't help it. I ask it every time. Mac answers every time, though he's gotta know I only ask it to hurt him now.

"How would I know?" he says, taking the bait.

"Gut feeling? Psychic energy? You feel her callin' for you?"

"Shit in the water can't talk."

"Whales can sing."

Mac pauses. "You think she could be a whale?"

"Nah. That's a mammal, not a fish. Doesn't fit."

"It's in the ocean, though. It's possible."

"None of the early ones were ever anything other than fish."

In the first years after the floods, you could tell when a fish was a fish and a fish was a human. Some of them had molars. Others had vestigial limbs, like toes or elbows on their fins, or cartilage where ears would fit. On others, their eyes rolled around like they were scared for their lives, begging me to fix them, or asking me to put them back. I never knew. None of them could talk. I ate the less human ones, but as

I ran out of food I started eating the ones a little more human. It wasn't so bad if you lopped off the person parts and gouged their eyes out of the way. Mac hated me then. We ate dinner in separate rooms, until all the fish started looking like fish, until they were indistinguishable. After that, Mac got over it enough to be around me, but not enough to enjoy the act of eating.

"Maybe it changed again," Mac says. "Maybe they're—"

"Maybe they're, maybe they're, maybe, maybe, maybe. If you keep maybe-ing you're gonna see the whole world as people, and then what are you gonna eat?"

About half a decade ago, Mac was drunk off his ass on rind wine when he told a story about sprinting down the Worcester train tracks to chase down a rat for dinner. That's how I learned he'd crossed miles of dry land on the way here. He could've eaten vermin to his heart's content, he still could if he up and left right now, but he would rather starve where his wife might be. I didn't bring it up. Easy to do when I didn't care about better shores anymore.

Mac shrugs. "I'll find something. Kelp. Algae."

"That's miles off the coast. We can't sail that far in a day."

"Then I'll make trips. I'll go out there for a week at a time, pile them up, and drag them back home on the back of the boat."

"Right, and the kelp will rot or the fish will eat it all, and you'll come back starved and delirious since you've got no food in the first place."

Mac says nothing.

"Mac, eat some jerky. You need some protein."

"Don't need it."

I don't push it. "Then some flour patties."

He does. His face makes it obvious it tastes bad. Disappointing. What a waste of good food.

"Any new theories?" Mac asks, onto the other thing we always talk about when we fish. He knows it humors me, keeps me occupied, keeps me from asking more about his wife. He's kind and he's selfish that way, just like me. I notice he's sweating and his forehead's red and I offer him my hat, which he takes after just a second of hesitation.

"Better not get lice off of you," he says.

"If I've got it, at least you'll have something else to eat."

Mac makes a face. "You tryna make me puke or tell me some stories?"

"I've got just two of them today," I say. "Tell me if you've heard this one already: chemical spill from—"

"You already said that. GMOs, right?"

"No, no, this is different. Chemical spill, but it's radioactive—"

"You said that too. Remember, you compared it to Fukushima."

"Okay, then not that one. But I'm sure the second is new."

"Why's that?"

I sigh. Mac's gonna be a bit too much of a tease about this one. "Because I started reading the Bible."

Mac laughs, just like I thought he would. I love hearing it. It's a rare sound these days, and he barely laughs to begin with. "*You*? What the hell do you get out of that?"

"It's fucking boring some days, ya know. You've got your jogging—crazy bastard, you should be saving calories, not wasting it—but all I've got is hanging around indoors."

"You could join me."

"Not a chance. I'm saving up until I've got a hundred years' worth in me," I say, patting my belly.

"You could read something else."

"If I see another one of those goddamn mystery novels left downstairs, I'll shoot myself."

Mac barks a laugh. "And now that you're godly, what do you figure about the good book?"

"The stories are fun. Just like movies. Like the wall of Jericho, all the shit Moses got up to, Noah, Solomon, the Queen of Sheba, Lot and his wife, what's her name—"

"She doesn't have a name."

"At all?"

"No, she's just Lot's wife. Looks back at him, turns to salt, same old story."

"Seems a shame. Doesn't get a name, but everyone else does."

"It's because she's an allegory for willpower, if you want to learn you gotta understand that—"

"I don't wanna learn. I just wanna read. Have fun. Occupy myself."

"It'd be good to have something to work at."

"I'm working on goddamn living. Get off my case, Mac."

To Mac's credit, he does. "So, your theory?"

"Armageddon, baby. It was Armageddon."

Mac doesn't say anything, so I think I'm onto something.

"So you know how Armageddon is about Jesus returning and the righteous getting raptured while the rest of us are left to suffer?"

"Yeah, I know."

"Imagine if Jesus was a fish, and heaven was the sea."

"And we're the only ones who aren't righteous?"

"Exactly."

"But we're . . . there's murderers and rapists and pedos and wifebeaters who got turned. But they were worth it?"

"By some fish standard, sure."

"We're good people."

"Speak for yourself," I snort. I'm not a bad person. I've stolen, I've lied, I've cheated, but I haven't done any of the big ones. Maybe except for envy, but in my opinion, that's not a big one.

"I'm a good man," Mac insists.

"Maybe, maybe not. I didn't know you," I say, bitter as spice.

"I worked hard, I was fair, I treated my neighbors well, and I loved my wife."

Again with her. My head is burning, black hair soaking in the heat like hot oil. Maybe that's why I change the topic. I do something that we never do on these fishing trips, but that I've done before on late nights, drunk nights, and mornings when I hate him and I hate myself. It's never ended well. I do it anyway.

"Tell me more about your wife."

"What do you care?" He's right. I don't care about her; I care about him, but I can't exactly say that.

"C'mon. We've known each other, probably longer than you were married to her. Don't I get something?"

"We knew each other twenty-three years," Mac murmurs. "Married for twelve."

I whistle. "Childhood sweethearts, then. That's something."

"Stop it. Don't push it."

"C'mon. All I know is that you love her, she's got green eyes, you hate talkin' about her, and you want her back. That's why we're out here, right?"

"I swear if you don't shut up."

"Gimme a name, a characteristic, something stupid about her laugh or her smile. About how you cared for her. She strikes me as a Cheryl or an Amy. Or maybe she was foreign? No, you're from here though, right, so how could she be a childhood sweetheart but also not from here?"

"Why the hell are you asking so many goddamn questions? You don't care about her, you've never met her."

*Well, maybe I want to know how you turned this way; what parts of you are parts of her, and vice versa.* I don't say that. I say, "Was she a looker? Curves up to here, legs down to there?"

"Shut up. I'm serious, shut up."

"She got a voice like velvet?" I croon, "Oh, Mac, baby, where'd you go? Fish me up, look me in my emerald eyes, and eat me like you used to—"

"Shut the *fuck up!*" Mac shouts, and he punches me in the face. It scares off any gulls that would have come close. I grab him by his collar, his shitty flannel shirt collar, awful plastic buttons on fraying threads popping off of the cotton as I rip it towards me. I'm bleeding, I can tell—it's getting all over my tee shirt. I'm swinging at him but not really trying to hit him, because even though I don't wanna hurt him I've gotta show him that I could and that maybe I want to, that I can be a man, that I can swing and hit and fight him even when I know I'm wrong and I've gone too far. He's not swinging anymore, his face is white and he knows he's fucked up, but he's clinging onto my arms like I'm his baby, like I could be his baby. We're yelling, we're rocking the boat, one of us is going to fall, and one of us might drown. If it's me, so be it. If it's him, I'll follow him down.

Then, the string on my pole goes taut. I push off of Mac and he lets go of me so I can move faster, so I can get the fish before it runs off. I try to reel it up and it's taking a while, the line whining more than usual, sounding like it might break. It's fighting me, I realize. It's trying to get away.

"Catch her!" Mac grabs my shoulders like I'm his life raft, like he needs to haul me back from falling over the boat, and he yells like a banshee, so loud that if the fish were at the surface they'd be scared off. Just when I wish he'd let go of me and stop shaking me around, he does, and then I miss him. He bends over the side of the boat, staring down into the water as if anyone could see more than a foot down.

"Come on, baby, come on. You were a fighter, you're a fighter now, it's you, it's gotta be you, I'm right here baby," he says into the water. He looks back up at me. "Reel her up already!"

"I'm fucking trying, Mac!" I yell. I consider letting go, losing all the line to whoever or whatever's down there. He's convinced every catch is his wife and every time I think he might be right, and that makes me want to quit fishing forever. I don't need it. I don't need to eat. I'll starve, waste away, all so we never have to find out what happens if—when, he thinks—we find her. Maybe he'll stop fishing and focus on finding a way to change her back. When he can't find anything to fix her up, he'll go crazy and start thinking people and fish are the same thing. Maybe he'll keep her in a bucket like a pet, feed her all the food he should be eating, and never look or speak to me again. He'll lift her from the water, forget to put her back, and she'll die, and he'll think he has no one left because he won't see me as someone. Some nights, I get scared thinking about what Mac will be like if that happens. I don't like it. I don't want to know what happens with us, what happens to me, so why do I have to help him get there? Why do I have to be the one to find his wife, to catch this fish?

I do, anyway, like I always do. It's a cod, two feet long, and Mac has to help me heft it into the cooler. I stare at him as he stares at the fish. He doesn't say anything, and eventually, he sits back at his pole. I do the same. Before sunset, we catch five more fish and no gulls. We head back home. Back on shore, he bandages my nose up for me but doesn't say anything. I know he feels bad beneath his sorry skin, so I take it. Even if he just feels bad because he didn't find his wife again or because he hates me, I take it. Him feeling bad is the closest thing to an apology I'll ever get.

Most of the catch goes into the smoker. I keep the cod for dinner, and as I get the cleaver out, I check the eyes, looking for flecks of green or humanity. Mac's gone up to his room to sulk, but if there was something in those eyes that he'd missed, I might have called him back down to check. I don't think it's her, I never do, but he might think differently. We might fight about it if he takes another look, gets another chance to convince himself of a delusion, and I don't want to have that fight again, so I just decide that I'm right.

I cut off the cod's head, filet it, and steam it with salt. Mac comes down during dinner, forgetting that he's got no more gull jerky yet again, and takes a couple of bites of my cod. He gags so hard when he swallows that I have trouble finishing the rest. He heads back to bed early, says he's tired. I say good night. He says it back. I'm alone. I regret pushing the issue like I do every time, but I know I'll do it again. Only way I'll stop is when one of us dies.

I take a bottle of the rind wine and sit on the balcony listening to the waves and watching the stars. I hear Mac snoring from the bedroom, from my bed, and I wonder if I could return there one of these days.

Mac thinks he'll know her when he sees her, but I don't. There's a million billion fish in the water. I think if we've found her, we've already eaten her, and if we haven't, we never will. I almost hope that he's right, that he would be able to tell her apart from the other fish. Maybe next time he takes a bite of my food, he'll notice it tastes like there's a drop of the perfume she used to wear or the musk of her sweat. I don't think it'll be good, what happens after that, but a little piece of me hopes that he'd just stop. He'd stop thinking about her all the time, stop searching for her, and she'd disappear from our lives. Sure, it'd take some time for him to get back to himself; I'd have to take even more care of him, make sure he remembered to eat, drink, and breathe, but he'd get back eventually. He'd come back to me, and then we could go back on our fishing trips. I think we'd like those trips more, then. No more searches. No one but the two of us. We could just fish for the sake of catching fish.

## ABOUT THE AUTHOR

**Tiffany Xue** is a biomedical engineer by day and writer by almost every other waking moment. Originally from New York, she now resides in Boston with her husband and their overgrown houseplants.

# Broken

## LAURA WILLIAMS MCCAFFREY

### VII

Flyer 247-3 hasn't flown in five days. In these five days, she has become accustomed to the hum and whine of the air filtration system cranked to its highest setting. She has become accustomed to her cell, four paces long, four paces wide. Its lack of view. She has become accustomed to peering through green goggles, to seeing the walls and most everything as yellow-green. Yellow-green walls, pantry door, front door, bathroom door, sink, water heater, reclining chair with its feeding IVs and other tubes and wires that she's usually hooked into through her suit. She is about to make all of this disappear.

She stands in her suit in front of her reclining chair, and she cradles her helmet, which she can't stop petting. The smoothness of it is the only sensation that makes this body feel anything other than heavy, as if the smoothness under her fingers transforms her to pure light.

Still, she hesitates. The shadow in the repair warehouse—what that shadow said. It was a joke, just a joke so the shadows could laugh at her behind her back. And the rest of what she saw outside her cell?

There must be some explanation.

So why hesitate?

She sits in the chair and fastens the suit to the tubes and wires. She lifts her helmet, the heavy hands of this body trembling. Finally, she can escape. Finally, she can return to the real world.

### VI

Flyer 247-3 hasn't flown in four and 3/4ths days. After the shadow sets down the box in her doorway, Flyer 247-3 wants to tear open the box. But she is not a fool.

The shadow walks away, and after Flyer 247-3 closes her cell's door, she fetches disinfectant from beside the sink. She returns to the box, and she sprays all of it, as well as the entire front door. Everything the shadow touched. She is, of course, wearing gloves. You can't be too careful. Then she puts the disinfectant aside. She kneels before the box. Her hands are shaking.

The box is sealed, and she fumbles, struggles to open it. Sweat drips down her forehead. *You don't need to lose water over this.*

She breaks the seal so suddenly that she loses her balance and sits back hard on her heels. She opens the box flaps.

The helmet lies nestled inside, glossy, black.

Her eyes leak.

She reaches under her goggles and wipes the wet. Then she touches the water to the helmet.

The helmet is worth her water. All her water.


## V


Flyer 247-3 hasn't flown in four and 1/2 days. There's a knocking sound from the door. Flyer 247-3 startles, then remembers yet again that shadows have to knock. They can't send or receive any kind of normal signal because they don't have helmets. And right now, neither can she.

The knock again.

She takes the four steps to the door. "Yes," she calls, her voice strange in her ears. It doesn't sound the way it does coming through her helmet's mic and speakers.

"Package," says a throaty voice. All shadows sound hoarse because they're outdoors a lot of the time and so breathe a lot of the unfiltered air. Through masks, but still.

She begins to shake. *Please, please be fixed.*

And be fine. She can't believe her commanders just let shadows carry helmets around. It makes her uneasy. This is one more thing that doesn't make sense.

That shadow in the warehouse is wrong though. The shadow in the warehouse has to be wrong.

She opens the door, caught off guard once again by the door's weight. She has to pull hard to actually open it.

The door swings open, and in the long dim hallway stands a shadow, their face and head entirely wrapped except for the eyes, which are behind goggles so dark she can't see through them. The shadow holds a box in their gloved hands.

"Set it down," she instructs, but the shadow tucks the box under one arm and extends a gloved hand. They make a gesture with their hand, so small that a few days ago she wouldn't even have noticed it.

The gesture—was it one?—is done, and the gloved hand is extended, palm up.

"Did you say something?" asks Flyer 247-3.

"Say something?" the shadow rasps. They sound completely perplexed.

"With your hand?" She points to the outstretched palm.

"I—You're supposed to pay for delivery," says the shadow. "They didn't tell you?"

Flyer 247-3 feels tricked—the shadow in the repair warehouse was making fun of her, pretending there was some kind of world she'd see if she just watched more closely. After she left, the shadow had probably told friends about tricking her. They all had probably laughed at her.

Wind comes through the hallway, from a briefly opened window or outer door somewhere, and rattles her cell door.

"No, I know I have to pay," she snaps. She stares at the open hand.

Right, of course. The shadow can't take real coin. There are metal coins in the emergency pouch under her chair. She doesn't want to leave her helmet in the hallway with the shadow. But she also doesn't want the shadow in her cell; she'll have to scrub everything they touch. She chooses the lesser of two evils. "One sec."

The shadow waits as she takes the steps to her chair, and she wishes she knew what the shadow is looking at. Then she's glad she doesn't know. Shadows are stuck inside those bodies all day and all night, their whole lives. Singular bodies that can't be sloughed off. Hungry and aching in the way that only a specific body aches. What must being trapped like that do to a person?

She opens the compartment under her chair. No emergency pouch.

Where did she put it? How does anyone keep track of anything when it isn't just there, the way it is in the real world? Maybe she left it in the rain wrap she wore to the repair warehouse?

She goes to the closet, where larger emergency items are, food packets, boots, the rain wrap, a fire extinguisher. Sitting on the top shelf is the emergency pouch. She opens it. There are three coins, but once they're lying in her gloved hand, they don't seem like enough for the delivery. They're small. They're dull, not shiny. She can't remember how much each one is worth, and until she has her helmet, there's no way to find out.

She grabs a food packet. Once she gets back to the real world, she'll have to ask for a restock of her emergency pouch and closet anyway. As long as the shadows and robots have definitely fixed her helmet, the tubes attached to her chair will work again, and she'll have the real food and the clean water she needs.

She returns to the shadow. "Here." She hands over the coins and the food packet.

The shadow stares down at the rectangular packet and the dull coins.

Flyer 247-3's knees tremble. It isn't enough. She won't get her helmet—her life—back.

Then the shadow says softly, "Fruit." Flyer 247-3 doesn't know what this means.

The shadow bows their head deeply; she's been generous somehow. The shadow hands over the helmet.

## IV

Flyer 247-3 hasn't flown in three days. She should care more about how the war with the Imperialists is going. Instead she just wants to crawl out of this terrible, terrible body and return to a place with beauty and with answers.

She does her daily calisthenics and weight training over and over, many more times than she usually does even though the absence of her helmet means she isn't doing calisthenics in beautiful places with friends or horses or whatever she wishes. The exercises are boring, and this body aches.

She is hungry from eating the mush packets full of strange tastes instead of drinking all her favorite tastes from the tubes attached to her chair. This body shakes. It craves.

It wonders things like, how does the food and water get restocked so it always comes out of the tubes? Where do the tubes lead? Somewhere in the building? Somewhere else further away? What did that shadow in the warehouse mean? What did what she saw in the warehouse mean?

This questioning, everything, is all temporary. Please, make it all temporary.

She considers strapping herself into the chair. Even without a functioning helmet, she can get the pulses of the chair to massage her. Would massage stop this shaking or worsen it? She doesn't know. She doesn't know.

The sound of the air filtration system scrapes her skin. The light coming from the globes in the ceiling stabs her eyes even though she's wearing goggles. Her throat is raw.

How can this be her body? It isn't her body.

She keeps grasping her knees. They seem too sharp and bony, not her. She doesn't remember ever feeling her knees before, the solidity of them, so how does she know they don't feel like her?

Does she remember what they felt like when she was little? She remembers the gray school, where they studied and took tests day after day. Then one day, a teacher said, "You're very good." They awarded her her first helmet. She wouldn't be a shadow.

Shadows know nothing. Everyone learns this young.

Shadows know nothing, and she isn't a shadow.

### III

Flyer 247-3 hasn't flown in two days.

After everything else she's tried, her only option seems to be taking the helmet to the repair warehouse herself.

Her commanders must know something's wrong with her, but she hasn't heard anything from anyone.

At the door that leads to the street, on the first floor of her building of cells, she stares through the window. Her cell doesn't have any windows, and she had forgotten about the flooding, the jungle breaking through the pavement when there isn't drought instead. Shadows appear and disappear, rising suddenly through the hazy air and then passing this building, swallowed by the haze beyond it.

She is dizzy from this body standing so much. This body, not her body.

She almost leans her head against the glass of the door. No. No touching here. She can so easily end up with flu or staph or a million other kinds of infection.

She has to row through the waterways, but it isn't until she's in a rowboat, her helmet safe in the backpack she wears, that she realizes rowing is much harder to do than she expected. Her calisthenics and other exercises haven't included rowing. She has to take many breaks and let the boat float a little. Waiting for the ache to lessen, she watches buildings drift past, huge concrete blocks with small or no windows, like the concrete block she lives in. Inside are fighters and flyers like herself, helmets on, soaring in the real world. Shadows keep passing her on the water, easily guiding their rowboats.

If she had realized how hard traveling this way would be, she would have hired one of the shadows to row her, after she figured out how. She does see shadows rowing people who aren't shadows. One or two are ill fighters or flyers, wearing helmets but lying back in the boats, emaciated, their skin dull. Maybe their chairs weren't feeding them properly or something. A few others whom shadows are rowing, she isn't sure what to make of them. Their rain suits have gold braid at the necks and are bright undulating silvers and golds. A boat full of such people turns down a waterway, and, in the distance, she sees a strange and huge building of white marble with gold glints. Its roof is turrets and spires. There was nothing like that here when she was a child, although she can't be entirely certain this is the same city where she was born. She's had to move buildings twice, and she had her helmet on the whole time, so she was in the real world while the move happened.

Even with that grand marble building as a destination, she doesn't understand why those people are traveling through this world. Who would stay in this world, with its tall gray buildings full of cells, its air full of smoky and salty water scents, its muddy water slopping over streets and buildings? In the real world, everything is cleaner and brighter, full of colors and wide spaces. You can lie in a garden and watch the stars on one day, and you can walk into any era you want the next day, to eat and drink, or to go to a show. You can play any game you want—epic sword fighting or racing through mazes, or anything, anything.

In the real world, her body moves however and wherever she wills. Its hurts are easy to soothe. Her body is mutable, hair color, skin color, the shape of her face, the sound of her voice. She can be a man or a little girl, an animal, whatever she wishes. She can be everything in the same day. She doesn't have a lot of time for romance and sex, but if she did, she could indulge however she wants—a girl who likes girls or guys or both, a guy who likes girls or guys or both, someone who is both or neither who likes anyone. She misses her flight partner, who is also most often a girl. She has always wanted to kiss her. What if now she never gets to?

In this body, she is stuck. One hair color, one skin color, one sound coming from her throat. Big hips, small boobs, 5 feet 3 inches tall. Her partner wouldn't even recognize her.

In the real world, she works a lot, and so doesn't often have free time, but she loves her work. In the real world, she flies and fights. Her heart rushes with the thrill of her life.

Right now, she feels so heavy and slow. She rows and hopes she hasn't stolen the boat. When she was a kid, rowboats were free, and you could simply take them, row to any dock, and leave them for someone to take next. But this world is different from the way she remembers it. There are those people in gold or silver, and their huge glittering building. She sees in the air—she's not sure. There are flying things, some shaped like small planes, others large and almost person-like, sleek. They fly so high up, she can't really make out what they are. More importantly, at the moment, some of the emergency instructions she had in her cell aren't right. They say nothing about her going to the repair warehouse herself; she was only supposed to go if called there. This world doesn't seem to work the way it's supposed to.

She rows, and her arms ache. The water's sheen here is iridescent. A lovely surface, but murky water beneath.

She reaches the warehouse's dock. It is right where the paper map from her emergency pouch said it would be, once she figured out how to read the map. The warehouse entrance must be at least two stories in the air. There's a long ladder.

As she climbs the ladder, it creaks and shudders in the wind. Her arms are so, so tired. Her calisthenics haven't helped her climb. Her eyes can't quite adjust to this world. Everything looks so flat here, or blurry far off and close up. It's not like the way things look on her helmet's screen.

She looks up, not down. She looks in the direction she's headed, not behind.

Once she's on the warehouse's platform, a light beside the door flashes. She's been scanned. Her commanders must now know she's here. They'll send someone to meet her. The door swings open.

The room she steps into is small and all smooth metal. She remembers the decontamination chambers from when she went to school in this world, and the jets start spraying. The liquid is so strong it scrapes her face. When the liquid stops, air or an air substance sprays from jets and pummels her. She's trapped in this body, and it hurts.

Another door opens. The room beyond is large, with a high ceiling that's two, maybe three stories up. A part of the upper level is glassed in and looks out over the rest of the huge room. Flyer 247-3 can't really see who or what is up there, but does see some bright gold and silver, orange and red. She is reminded of the people she saw being rowed by the shadows. On the level where she stands, each wall is covered with shelves, and lines of shelves fill the middle of the room. On each shelf sit boxes, also metals and wires, bolts and nails, hoses and molded plastics. She remembers what these are from when she was in school. In one section of the room stand reclining chairs like her own. Lots of things don't look familiar, piles of pieces.

At many tables stand shadows and robots, but the robots are different than the ones in the real world. They are large and tall, with many dexterous arms and prism-like heads. The robots seem to be doing a lot of the work on whatever machine lies on the table, but instead of assisting the shadows, they seem to be assisted by the shadows. Commands play from the speakers where mouths would be on a human face. The shadows do precise work, holding narrow or small tools. A robot beeps, and another robot commands a shadow to flip a tiny switch on the table, which stops the beeping. Flyer 247-3 gapes.

When she was at school, robots were smaller and servile. In the real world, robots are smaller and servile. They help people, not the other way around. People do the most interesting and important work.

This body, something feels wrong with this body. She feels dizziness, and her skin prickles. She is chilly.

She is standing just inside the door, and no one seems to notice her. Her commanders—they're not here.

She takes a step forward, and a bell chimes. A shadow off to the right walks over. Though the shadow is inside, its face and head are still wrapped, and it wears gloves. None of its skin shows.

It raises a gun. Flyer 247-3 reaches for hers, and grasps nothing; she doesn't have a gun here. Only in the real world. Both her hands raise, palms open in a sign of surrender. This body's heart is racing, and its chest is tight. She scans the room for an escape route.

With its free hand, the shadow points to one of Flyer 247-3's. She has an old memory of holding out her wrist, a gun pointing at it and flashing so she could enter the school. She extends one hand, wrist turned up. The shadow points the gun and pulls the trigger. The gun flashes. A slender light briefly illuminates under her skin.

The shadow looks at the gun's display. "Missing." Its voice is a harsh whisper. "Two days."

"You didn't already know?" Flyer 247-3 asks. "Is that why no one came? I waited. Then I had to use the emergency plans, but they weren't up-to-date. I didn't know how to get here."

Instead of an explanation, the shadow gives the slightest shake of the head. But maybe Flyer 247-3 might be imagining it. Plus it gives a small wave of the fingers. Derision?

Flyer 247-3 says, "Something must be wrong if you didn't already know I'd blipped out." She resists the urge to ridicule the paper map and the confusion about the boats. This shadow has never seen the real world, and the many kinds of maps there that show up in front of you, the way you can just ask with your mic and get answers to anything right before your eyes. The shadow doesn't know how much more there is.

The shadow says, "Well?"

Flyer 247-3 takes her helmet out of the sack, and then she hands it to the shadow. The shadow turns the helmet to look at the back. Pointing the gun at the helmet, it pulls the trigger again, and the gun flashes. The shadow studies the reader's panel.

Behind the shadow, robots roll past, disregarding them, as if Flyer 247-3 is completely unimportant. Too unimportant to notice. As if *their* noticing is what makes something important.

Flyer 247-3 can't stop looking at the robots. They don't have legs, instead a kind of base that's flared wider at the bottom and seems to have wheels that turn and swivel. Some have two arms, some have more, as many as eight. They seem to have two fronts; they can work on both sides, the arms adjusting to reach in any direction. Their heads, chests, and backs are multifaceted. Like insect eyes? They can see from all those panes. Some, one at each table, has a marking on the shoulder, star shapes that remind her of the patches her commanders have on their uniforms.

In the real world, Flyer 247-3 barely thinks about robots. They are mindless, useful but insignificant. The way they were when she was a kid. Here, they seem, not human but—what? Sentient?

Flyer 247-3 notices that the shadows keep their heads bowed and work without pause. They don't speak. Like robots in the real world.

Flyer 247-3 glances toward the upper floor. Up there, those in gold and silver must be people. They have to be, but why would they let robots command any person, even a shadow—that makes no sense.

Flyer 247-3 feels she has fallen into a mirror. Everything is the wrong way around.

The shadow before her has flipped her helmet over. It pops open a panel.

"What's wrong?" Flyer 247-3 asks. "Can you see?"

The shadow ignores her. It holds the helmet near its face and looks closely.

"Is my helmet all right?" What if she is stuck in this wrong-way-around world where she can't seem to get any answers?

"Just a routine check for sabotage," the shadow rasps, sounding like it has said this a million times.

Flyer 247-3 is shocked speechless. Then she says, "I didn't wreck it."

"I'm sure," rasps the shadow but it doesn't sound like it cares one way or the other. "Cyber sabotage. Sometimes you can see the damage."

Flyer 247-3 touches the back of her head, about where the panel must touch her when she wears the helmet. "I did hear some sensors ping. Could it have been malware? Have the Imperialists broken into our systems? Do you see anything?"

"The sensors I can read aren't showing much, but that doesn't mean the higher-ups won't find something. It's a game of cat and mouse." The shadow sounds tired. "They'll upgrade your sensors."

Flyer 247-3 says, "The Imperialists can damage the helmet itself, get that close to this head?" Unlike all her other heads and faces in the real world, here, she only has one. If it's gone, it's gone. She's gone, which feels odd to think. This place is so unimportant.

The shadow is silent. The wrap around its head, the layers, folds, and twists, obscure its features, but also, Flyer 247-3 realizes that if she looks into the dark gap where there should be eyes, she can see eyes. She stares. The shadow stares back.

Flyer 247-3 feels an odd sense of familiarity, of recognition. Did she know this shadow before she became a flyer in the real world? Back at school, when she was little?

The shadow does a strange thing. They breathe, "Are you sure you're fighting the Imperialists?"

She is confused. Does the shadow think she's from a different division? "I am—I, what I'm doing is classified?" She assumed all the information was there on that reader, but apparently not. "I shouldn't have said anything." She's suddenly glad her commanders aren't here.

The shadow gives something like a laugh. "*I'm* the one who doesn't know who you're fighting."

Flyer 247-3 steps back. This is like nothing she's ever encountered in the real world. She doesn't even know what to call it. She needs to get the helmet fixed so she can get answers. She needs to get back to all the people who know her and who understand how the world works. "When will my helmet be done?"

"When it's done," says the shadow. "Go back to your cell, and it'll be delivered."

*By a shadow?* She's a little shocked by this but the shadow is the wrong person to say it to, and she doesn't have anyone else to ask.

As she hovers, frightened the helmet will never make it back to her, the shadow says, "You know—" The whisper is so soft, she thinks she might be imagining it. "They can make almost anything look like anything else. But the newest malware attacks go after the skins. When the skins break up, even a little, you should pay attention to what the skins are hiding."

Flyer 247-3 almost spits, *They're not "skins," they're bodies! And what the hell are you talking about? Who is your supervisor? I want to talk to your supervisor.*

But the shadow has already turned their back on her and is walking to a robot. The shadow's head bows as they show the robot the reader gun and the helmet. The robot takes these with hands that are more like clamps or magnets than five fingers and a palm. The robot makes a sound, and the shadow, head bowed, turns away, walking toward a table with tools on it.

Flyer 247-3 feels queasy.


## II

Flyer 247-3 hasn't flown for one day. She can't wait any longer for someone to come fix her helmet. Why hasn't anyone come?

Here, there is a quietness in her head. An aloneness. In the quiet is a question voice that isn't usually there. It asks, it asks, it asks, *How will you get back to the real world?* No other voices. Just that one echoing.


## I

"Flyer 247-3 in position," she reports to her squad. She loves this part, the speeding rush toward a fight. She feels she is sparking. She is warm, perfectly warm. She is bright.

The music in her ears pounds a rapid beat. It swells as the landscape spills endlessly through her monitor. The snow-capped peaks. The yellow-orange and red rock faces, epically tall and jagged. Even though there's so much fighting, the land is still beautiful, worth battling for and protecting.

A forest of lush blue-green trees stretches below, then a mountain lake of clear sparkling aqua.

"Punch it," says one of her commanders right in her ear. She loves this too, that voice louder than the music, all the voices always with her. In her monitors, all the planes together speed over the lake.

The plateau is ahead. She can see it now, and their job is to take it back. It is a rich red, and she can see that there are houses on it, as well as huge gardens of wildflowers, blue, red, yellow, orange. The Imperialists can't keep it; her heart fills with the need to liberate it.

"No sign of engagement forces. We have to hit 'em fast before they can use any anti-aircraft fire."

She, with the rest, all affirm they've heard this, many voices forming one voice. Yes, yes, yes.

They swoop lower, and she can make out the flower gardens, a stone fountain shaped like swans holding a basin. No one on the streets. The Imperialist forces must have taken over the houses. She waits for the order to prepare the bombs.

Then, as she's approaching one of the biggest houses, Imperial forces stream out, a number of Imperialists rolling a huge gun. The music in her ears is loud, fast, and her heart syncs to the rhythm. More Imperialist soldiers spill out of the houses. The Imperialists must have bad intel. They must think there are ground troops to fight. Her speakers are a little staticky for a moment. She sees a weird glitch. It's like the Imperialist soldiers' guns are floating but their hands aren't holding the guns.

Everything suddenly starts rising up the screen, distorting and smearing. She hears the pings of sensors sounding alerts, but no explanatory message plays.

Everything she sees is wrong. Her instruments are pixelated. Her own arms and hands, her body, pixelates.

"This is Flyer 247-3. I'm—" She doesn't know what she is.

The answer is garbled, metallic sounds.

She stabilizes. Her screen clears. Imperialist soldiers. Guns floating. Hands floating. The guns flicker. The people's arms are raised above their heads. Their hands, their palms, open.

Her screen goes black.

"This is Flyer 247-3." Her voice is harsh and doesn't come through the speakers. "This is Flyer 247-3."

"Something's wrong!" she cries. "Something's broken!"

"Something's broken!"

Silence. Darkness.

She is alone.

She lifts off the helmet, and she blinks, confused, in the light.

## ABOUT THE AUTHOR

**Laura Williams McCaffrey**'s short stories have appeared in *Cicada, Solstice Literary Magazine,* and *YA Review Network,* earning such honors as the SCBWI Magazine Merit Award. She's also published three YA fantasy novels with Clarion Books, *Marked, Water Shaper,* and *Alia Waking.* She teaches at Solstice, the low-res MFA program at Lasell University, and at Cabot School, a small K-12 school. She lives in a little house in the Vermont woods with her musician husband.

# How to Remember Perfectly
## ERIC SCHWITZGEBEL

Joy catches my eye, shuffles my direction. Her face lights the dining room. Her curly gray hair is the sun's corona, and she seems to float above her walker, needless of her stiff little legs. In seeming slow motion she arrives at the seat across from me.

Eating and conversation have stopped. Everyone is transfixed—even the Sunrise Senior Living staff—as if by gazing upon Joy we could sample her emotional enhancement, her technologically installed wisdom and delight. Yesterday she trembled with grief, but today she soars. Apart from a few stray clinks as we unenhanced ordinary octogenarians lower our forks, the room is silent.

Joy settles into her seat, then leans across the table toward me. "I fully comprehend Donald's life and death," she whispers. Her husband's memorial flowers and plaque are still visible at the dining room entrance. "I am complete and perfect in this moment, without need. Time and self are only forms we project onto the world. The past is but a habit of thought."

If she notices my ambivalent reaction to this strange speech, she gives no sign. I reply also in a whisper, "Yes, Joy, you are complete and perfect. If divinity could take human form, it would be you today." At the tail end of life, we enjoy gin rummy, reruns of *Seinfeld,* and soft serve ice cream in palm-sized bowls. And of course our memories—our *real* memories, unaltered, unenhanced. Shouldn't this be enough?

Joy and Don used to sit with me every day at this time for an early dinner. Starting last week, it was Joy alone, but never like this. The low sun slants orange across the unoccupied balcony, through the tall windows.

Though Joy and I remain still, activity resumes around us. Joy smiles at me, beneath large, pink-rimmed glasses. Her eyes seem bright with life—warm, accepting, energetic, as if seeing me anew and better. Her ancient hands encircle a glinting water glass but do not yet lift it.

I lie on my back in bed at 9:30 p.m., in a pleasant drowse as the sleep medicine begins to take me. The dry, warm wind of central heating brushes my face. I recall footage from a nature documentary I had watched an hour before: In the shallows of a wide African river, a mother elephant had pulled her baby elephant from the teeth of a crocodile. I turn my mind to death.

My daughter Robin, dead in a motorcycle accident. I picture her crouched low in black leathers, doing 85 mph on a wide freeway through the dry foothills southeast of Oakland. A two-by-four angles across her lane, which she notices too late. She hits it. Her bike lies flat, a footpeg sparking on the concrete. She floats up in a low parabola ahead of her bike, then strikes the lane and tumbles. A white delivery truck hits her.

My husband Anil. He spent nineteen years fighting three cancers, until he was bony and gray-skinned, unable to stand without help, a skeleton with a pulse. He faded away rather than dying of anything in particular.

Joy's husband Donald, last week, in his sleep. Stooped and confused by the end, unsure whether he'd eaten, needing to be pointed the right direction in the hallway to and from the dining area—but always with a sharp tie and hat, like a 1940s movie star.

There's an ascetic purity, isn't there, in the bald truth, in the sadness, in the loneliness? A rigor in the fixed lines of the past.

Yet I didn't actually see Robin die. I don't know how her bike fell or the color of the truck that hit her. I imagine it a particular way, until my imagination seems to become the truth—a beautiful truth, almost: her moment of soaring free, suspended timeless in my memory.

Joy is at my door. We watch TV together. There's little need to talk. We sit, each in our own thoughts, but together—a friendship comfortable with silence. Since her enhancement began, she has become somehow both more attentive and more spacey, more immediately present and more remote, as if she saw and understood everything more precisely but contemplated it more privately. She has not tried to explain it to me.

Today she shows me a joystick.

We are hip to hip on my loveseat, facing the large TV monitor across the room. At our knees is an elegant, tiled coffee table I inherited from my father. Her legs are floral skirted, while I wear green slacks. Joy lifts the joystick in her papery hand, turning it in the light as if examining a piece of fruit. Its light-gray casing is marked with four symbols: an up arrow, a down arrow, a dark ring on the left, a blazing sun on the right. Atop the stick is a single blue button.

She hands it to me. "Gently," she says.

I nudge the handle toward the up arrow.

"Pleasure," she says, pivoting with some effort and easing herself back against the pillowed arm of the loveseat, using her arms to manually lift and rest her stiff legs across my lap. She smiles and looks at me.

I let the stick return to center. Joy closes her eyes and her breathing slows. I nudge the stick a little toward the down arrow.

"Sweet sadness," she says. "For everything we have lost. For everything we have yet to lose." She is still smiling, but her smile has changed.

I nudge the stick toward the dark ring.

"Relaxation," she says. She is almost melting into the maroon cushions. "The longer you hold it, the longer it will last after you return the stick to center."

I pause a few seconds, then let the stick return to center. "And the sun?"

"I could doze here," she says. "Or you could brighten me. Don't press the blue button yet. We'll save the guided crafting."

I brighten her. A millimeter at a time, I nudge the stick up and right, mixing the up arrow and the sun. Joy slowly raises her arms, stretching her palms toward the ceiling. Her fingers straighten, her elbows lock, her back arches—then she opens her eyes, lowers her arms, and looks steadily at me. She is radiant, an angel aglow.

She studies me seriously through those adorable, pink-rimmed glasses. "For a very long time I have wanted to kiss you," she says.

I have not kissed anyone since Anil died nine years ago. I had assumed I was done with kissing. It had simply not occurred to me that the possibility existed. My last kiss had been on Anil's eerily cool forehead, ninety minutes after his death, his soft body at unmammalian room temperature, the crematory man standing ready to zip him into a black bag and haul him away.

I gaze down on Joy's bare shins—pale landscapes irrigated by delicate blue veins, flowered with flecks of brown and red. I find them beautiful.

Joy manually lifts her legs again, pivoting around and setting her feet on the floor. She turns back to face me, then folds her hands around my hands, which still hold the controller. She guides my fingers slowly away from the joystick, letting it drift again toward center. She sets it down on the coffee table. I hear the click of the heater engaging. I smell a sweet, medical, old-woman smell.

I have always been slow to notice the affection of others, slow to understand that love might be directed my way, uncomprehending of what about me another person could find attractive. But even I could not mistake the message of Joy's eyes. Some long-closed part of me begins to open.

I lean forward for her kiss and we are young again.

Jeremy Bentham's felicific calculus mathematizes the meaning of life: Add all the pleasures and subtract all the pains. Pleasure is the only intrinsic good. Pleasure alone requires no excuse. An event is choiceworthy to the extent it creates pleasure, *pro tanto* and *ceteris paribus*. Everything else is only derivatively good—good instrumentally, as a means or method, direct or indirect, of increasing pleasure or reducing pain. A photograph is good because it brings you joy. An income is good because you can use it to avoid the pain of hunger or to purchase the pleasure of a vacation. Justice is good because it promotes a happy society.

"This mathematical philosophy should appeal to you as—if I'm remembering correctly—a former high school geometry teacher," suggests Doctor Pinkbeard, with a wink.

Joy had encouraged me to meet the doctor. She thought the doctor might persuade me to join her in enhancement—an expensive experimental procedure, for which she would gladly help pay. What other use did she have for her wealth?

The doctor looks barely twenty-five. He has a shiny forehead and unkempt blond hair in a long ponytail—plus a giant bushy dyed beard, the source of his nickname, which he is constantly running his fingers through.

I have already decided, but I want Pinkbeard to earn it. "That philosophy might appeal to an algebraist. But we geometers appreciate the beauty of multidimensional form, which cannot be captured in a simple sum."

"Beauty is a thing's propensity to induce an appreciative reaction," replies the doctor. He spins around in his rolling stool and pulls a surgical mask from a drawer, holding it aloft between finger and thumb. "Beauty too can be enhanced. If you tune your mind just right, so that you really see this mask—really *see* it, not just bounce your eyes across it, as ordinary people mostly do—it would astound you with its beauty. So blue and white! Its fibers, so perfect. Its functionality, so benign. The art of generations of nurses and doctors, manufacturers and shippers and salespeople, packaged in plastic, nourished by custodians! But of course it is not just this mask, it is everything in this room and everyone you meet. Beauty gathers in everything, if you are ready to sense it." He seems earnest. His nose appears soft, strangely delicate, as if I could knead it into a new shape.

"Isn't it illusion, though? To judge always so positively? The packaging will become landfill. The mask's manufacture and shipping harm the environment. It is one of a million identical disposable items, made without human touch. It symbolizes all the risks and suffering of the hospital."

"You are right, of course," says Doctor Pinkbeard. "This is why I have not enhanced myself. It is, to a substantial extent, illusion." He presses his black sneakers against the linoleum floor and his rolling stool glides backwards across the room, away from me. He stands and begins typing on a keyboard with his right hand, while his left hand scrunches his beard. He is no longer looking at me, almost as though he has forgotten me.

My legs are uncomfortable from sitting on the high patient's table, my feet dangling without support. I try shifting my weight to the right, but this draws a twinge of pain from my hip.

"Would you like a harmonica, Mx. Sung?" says the doctor, pulling one from the pocket of his scrubs.

I look at him, puzzled. A harmonica?

"I bought my son six for his birthday, but he doesn't want them." Doctor Pinkbeard smiles and bounces his shoulders around a few times. He seems torn between keeping a professional demeanor and revealing that he's really just a puppy who wants to play. The medical world is his chew toy.

"Okay," I say.

The doctor glides back over to me on his rolling stool, harmonica in his outstretched hand. "If you blow a low E, you might hear the harmonies of the universe. I think you could teach your friend Joy."

A hundred thousand dollars. A hundred thousand dollars could feed so many children. It was self-indulgent, I had told her.

*Our living here at all is self-indulgent,* Joy had replied. *So many people care for us, and we contribute nothing. Should we not exist at all, then? Or does something reside in us that is still worth cultivating?*

Yes, yes, I had conceded. But worth cultivating in what way?

"You haven't mentioned changing my memories, 'improving' them," I tell the doctor.

Doctor Pinkbeard looks fixedly at me, pressing both hands down on the sides of his stool, elbows locked, shoulders forward. His beard seems to cover his whole narrow, boyish chest. "That is correct. I haven't. Of course the functionality is there, should you choose it."

A large clear jar waits on the procedure room counter. It contains a pale blue gel.

"The first step would be those nanites," says the doctor. Did he just wink at me again or was it a trick of the light?

I press the blue button of Joy's controller, and she presses mine. We are on my maroon loveseat, facing each other, our backs to the pillowed arms, knees touching. Doctor Pinkbeard is watching us through the television monitor.

The brain contains a hundred trillion synapses, a billion in every cubic millimeter of the cortex. These synapses are about thirty nanometers wide, often with vast micrometers of usable volume around them—ample room for a few trillion protein-sized nanites to snuggle in. The blue button is doing its magic: I can feel my mind expanding, gaining the neuroplasticity of a baby. The world grows bright and yummy. Everything wants my attention, and my attention is a lantern that illuminates it all effortlessly, without competition or distraction, as easily as the sun lights the surface of the sea. I am a buddha, I am a newborn child, I am the fissioning center of the cosmos. We two, Joy and I, are equal centers. Her face is an entire planet, her secret depths the radioactive core. I am alive to new possibilities, new realities.

We will craft a memory.

For our guided crafting, we have chosen the most incandescent of cities, Las Vegas. "We drove in my old red car, through the hot desert night, windows down, smoking cigars," I say. And it is true, we drove in my old red car, through the hot desert night, windows down, smoking cigars. It is not true, but it is true.

"The city is an electric flower, growing on the horizon as we approach," says Joy. And the city is an electric flower, growing on the horizon as we approach.

"I pull over on a dark side road. I am so high from cigars that I need to vomit! I barf into an empty ditch. Nothing could be more glorious than to barf into a ditch. Immediately, my stomach calms and my mind is clear." And it is true, nothing could be more glorious than to barf into a ditch. This is the Buddha's wisdom, the Daoist insight, the consensus of the Andromedean sages that hypothetically exist.

"I hold your waist as you vomit," says Joy, "and in that moment I could love nothing more than you, barfing. Then we are back in the car."

Piece by piece, we construct the perfect vacation. It becomes true. A shared memory. Something Don let her do, lovable, generous Don. We fit the new vacation into our understanding of the past, making it real. No one can tell us it isn't so.

We kiss, and Doctor Pinkbeard signs off with a chuckle, saying "I think you two can take it from here."

We have always kissed, for years and years we have been kissing. It is not true, but it is true.

Joy's apartment has pictures and pictures, the walls are crowded with pictures, never have I seen so many. Joy and Don. Don. Joy and Don. Politicians she has met (she had been a political reporter). Ancient college photos. Her long-ago roommates. A prom photo. Friends from middle age, none of whose names I know. Places she has been: New York, Paris, the Great Barrier Reef, horseback riding in Mongolia, the islands of Greece, a tour-guide holding up a stone with the melting glaciers of Iceland behind him. Thirty-five-year-old Joy in a sleek sportscar. Cousins, uncles, her uncles' wives, children of her cousins. Pictures from the early twentieth century, people long dead, staring at the camera, thinking who knows what, remembering who knows what.

Joy's apartment is a large two-bedroom, one of the best at Sunrise, with a view over oak trees and across vineyards. It is a jumble of floral couches, lacy end tables with mother-of-pearl lamps, mahogany ledges with statuettes crafted by regional artists, intricately carved bureaus, decorative tea sets, ceilings tacked with Indian patterned cloth—so feminine, as if no man had ever lived there, except for an incongruous exercise bicycle in one corner. Even when Donald was alive, it had been this way. He and his neat hat had always seemed to just fit in the corners. He hardly said a word but always belonged, like a habitual and preternaturally comfortable guest.

I am on Joy's bed, leaning back on lacy pillows while she sits in a soft armchair, my controller in her hand. She brightens me—pure bright, no up arrow, no down arrow. There is a whole world in that crystal-cased overhead light. The light glows and bends prismatically through glass gems, light born a few nanoseconds ago in the LED, light born eight minutes ago in the Sun, invisible light that has been traveling timeless since the Big Bang. I seem to hear exactly where each bird is, outside among the oaks, as if I can place them precisely each on a branch. Every fiber of my clothing excites my skin.

"Think of Anil," she says.

Anil teaching Robin to drive. A big brown car with stained fabric and sun-bleached paint. I am in the back seat. Robin cannot keep to her lane, is scared of the center, is almost sideswiping the parked cars on her right. I am tense, not wanting to say anything but about to say something. How should I phrase it? Robin always prickles at criticism.

"You idiot," says Anil. "You're going to hit those fucking cars." There's a red bump on the back of his neck, which we don't yet know is cancer, the first of his cancers.

Robin jerks the car left, too far, almost into the oncoming traffic, and I surge with fear.

All this is bright, vivid, real, real, as real as if I were living it again.

"Make it better," says Joy, softly. She must see how tense I am. I feel her press the blue button—I feel it as an opening up of spaces in my mind, as if my synapses are expanding, changeable, eager for something new.

Anil teaching Robin to drive. A big brown car with stained fabric and sun-bleached paint. I am in the back seat. Robin keeps so smoothly to the center of the lane—a natural. We wait to turn left at a red light. It turns green and Robin steers slowly into the intersection, but too sharply, aiming head-on at the stopped cars on the wrong side of the divider. Nothing sudden. She is cautious, confused. She presses the brake, and we stop in the middle while the drivers in the waiting cars stare at us, slowly figuring out what's going on.

"See those drivers?" Anil says. "They are taxpayers. They have paid good money to use that side of the road. They don't want you to hog up their side when you already have your own side, right there waiting for you." He points, "That way."

Robin snorts and slowly steers the car to the correct side of the divider.

A much better memory. Has Joy pushed a bit on the up arrow? A taste of pleasure, not too much, the right amount. So real, so lovely. It is the new picture in my mind. It is how Anil was. It is how Robin was. It is the new truth.

Magic too is real. In the back of my closet is a door to Faerie, which Joy and I can crawl through.

To celebrate this idea, we are drawing the door on the rear closet wall. To give us room to work, we've emptied the space. My colorful slacks and coats and my white Oxford button-down shirts are heaped on my queen bed. The mirrored closet door is open wide. I have helped Joy down onto her hands and knees, and we kneel with our heads in the closet, markers uncapped, like kindergarteners. I have drawn and shaded the faerie door in brown. Joy rims it with flowers. I draw a demon-face knocker. Joy writes "O Beautiful Hell!" in elegant letters. I surround the faerie door with smiley faces, stars, and swirls in yellow, blue, and green. Joy draws long, colorful arrows pointing toward the door. In small letters near the floor, on the far side of the closet, I write "Now hold on a minute, is it a trap?"

It is no trap. We ride dragons. We climb mountains. We dance with elves. We rescue knights and ally with maidens. She is a princess, and I am her page. We shrink to the size of dragonflies and drink the nectar of roses. We ride the shoulders of cloud giants. I am a unicorn and she is the merry bandit who captures me. We sit by tide pools at sunset, side by side. We catch raindrops on our tongues. I have studied for years and am now a mighty wizard, called by the king to save the land. We lie on our backs in a flowery field, while ants tickle us.

It is all real. How perfectly we remember! I pity you unbelievers, who will never have the key to our door.

Strong, strong Anil. What took him in the end? He had a heart attack in bed, never saw it coming. He had been a jogger, a cyclist, a brilliant lawyer. On late weekend mornings I welcomed him home sweaty from his exercise, and we made love. On weekdays, we would cook dinner together, pork fried rice, burned just right, or sweet corn chowder, or a barely seared whole fish. How well I remember.

Robin had moved to Bhutan in her twenties. She became a monk in the mountains. She wrote long, joyful letters, describing the scenery, the snow, the wild yaks, the many weird characters in the monastery, the surreal politics of Bhutan's benevolent monarchy. Why don't I have any of those letters? Because . . . because . . . I burn them after reading. I burn them, for memory is always more perfect than black words on a page. Memory has a sweet haziness to it, don't you agree? I picture Robin floating, as if the mountains were removed but she is still at elevation, meditating in harmony with the cosmos, suspended timeless.

I can't seem to shake the idea that Anil's forehead was oddly cool to the touch, as if he were secretly empty. But everything is empty, after all: There is no essential self, only swirling patterns of causation. Moment to moment, there is only the present and whatever you choose to make of the past and the future. To realize this is to cease suffering.

Joy is in the hospital. I am playing poker in the Sunrise Living game room, with four old men plus Eve, who I think might have been a bullfighter in a previous life. For four days, I have not touched my joystick—not since the screaming ambulance hauled Joy away.

"Welcome to reality," Bernd had said, when I had staggered into the room, much less bright than usual. "The cards will break your heart."

In truth, the men are terrible at poker and it's lucky for them that we only play for nickels. We play a few hands.

"Any news about Joy?" asks Hunter. Hunter is as round as a frog, and almost as green. He wears plaid, but I forgive him. He looks at me as if I might be a fly.

My hole cards are six and seven of clubs. The flop brings a five of clubs and a couple of diamonds, face up in the center of the table. I study my hole cards carefully, noting each bend in the thirteen black flowers which we have agreed to call "clubs." My downcast eyes are answer enough for Hunter.

Eight of clubs on the turn, the fourth up card. One more club would give me a flush. A four or a nine in any suit would give me a straight, but I don't want to think about it. When the bet comes around, I push in the maximum—twenty nickels in four neat stacks.

"Bold!" says Eve.

On the wall, the same old print as always: Petals floating down a stream, point of view just a few centimeters above the water, one petal almost touching, it seems, the viewer's eye. Bernd calls, matching my bet.

The final up card, the river, is a queen of spades. Nothing. I push in five nickels, but Bernd knows I don't have it. His nothing beats my lower nothing.

"The cards will break your heart," he says. He is swimming in my vision. The room is tilting.

I still have the key to Joy's apartment, which Sunrise had forgotten to collect from Don when he died. I let myself in and sit on her couch without turning on the lights. Everything is motionless. I sit doing nothing, not even thinking.

No, that's not right. I am thinking of Joy, of Robin, of Anil, of that boy I knew in high school, of classrooms full of geometry kids whose faces blur into each other. But my thinking is slow like honey.

I have brought Doctor Pinkbeard's harmonica. I had laid it in a drawer and forgotten about it. I had forgotten to show it to Joy. I hold the harmonica aloft, noticing how its metallic surface mirrors and distorts the room. I do not blow.

I am in Doctor Pinkbeard's procedure room for the weekly checkup on my experimental nanites. Joy has been in ICU for eight days, and I haven't been permitted to see her. Only kin will be admitted, but she has none who are close enough to attend to her situation.

A stray surgical mask is on the procedure room counter, and I try to imagine it as a pinnacle of beauty. I have my joystick, so I know I could imagine the whole cosmos in that mask, if I wanted to.

A middle-aged woman in blue scrubs enters the room. "I'll be your doctor today," she says. "How have you been feeling?"

"Where is Doctor Pinkbeard?" I ask.

"Oh, honey, don't you know?" She tilts her head at me sympathetically.

"Don't I know what?"

"Doctor Pinkbeard died last weekend in a sailing accident."

I picture Doctor Pinkbeard standing on the edge of a sailboat, barefoot in a blue Speedo, eyes closed in delight, smiling in the wind, beard flying. The boom swings violently around, slams the side of his face, and he falls in the water. I imagine him sinking headfirst in the ocean, deeper, deeper into the darkness, his pink beard spreading like a sea anemone.

Joy has been removed from life support. She asked for me, and they are permitting me some time with her. My joystick is in her hands and hers is in mine.

"The faerie door was real?" she asks, looking at me like a child and at the same moment like a corpse.

"As real as anything, Joy."

"You were the unicorn I captured? The wizard?" She grins weakly.

Can I say this to her? I am confused myself.

"Aw, it was just pretend," she says. "But sweet, sweet pretense! More intense than life itself. Did we ever kiss? Was that real?"

It has always been real. I kiss her wrist. I kiss her lips. I kiss her forehead.

"Don loved me?"

"So many questions! Soon you will need no more answers." How much she has remade her memories of Don, I have no idea. "He never would have let us go to Vegas like that, though!"

"I think I need to vomit," she says.

"Nothing could be more glorious than to barf into a ditch," I reply. From my pocket I pull Doctor Pinkbeard's harmonica and blow a low E. It resonates off the cabinets, off the linoleum floor, it seems to buzz through my whole body.

"It is time, I think, for the bright depths," Joy says.

I pocket the harmonica, then lift her joystick. She keeps mine in her lap. Slowly, in synchrony, we move them down and to the right, maximizing the down arrow and the sun. We fill with a radiant energy of tears, and all the death of the world is vivid for us at once, the dead trees in the cabinetry, the ancient, fossilized shells in the calcium carbonate of the linoleum, the melted and purified rock in the steel railings of her

41

bed, our own deaths, the past or future deaths of everyone we know. It is exaggerated, I know it is exaggerated, but I crave the exaggeration. It is artificial wisdom, but real wisdom has eluded us. Age has not taught us what we really want to know.

Slowly, I nudge the stick away from the sun and toward relaxation. Joy follows my lead, looking at me. When I pause, she pauses too. Then she nods to me to keep going, and I tilt her stick toward darkness while she releases mine. She seems to welcome it, though not with the smile I'd been hoping for. She falls asleep. Her breath ceases.

I place her joystick in her lap and fold her dead hands around it. I take possession again of my own joystick. I have no impulse to use it. Something in me closes, darkens, hardens. I stiffen in my seat and stare at the cabinets, seeing nothing.

## ABOUT THE AUTHOR

**Eric Schwitzgebel** is a professor of philosophy at University of California, Riverside, and author of over a hundred academic articles in philosophy, psychology, and technology ethics. His stories have appeared in *Clarkesworld, F&SF, Nature,* and *The Dark* and his op-eds in *The Atlantic, Salon, Slate,* and the *Los Angeles Times.* If you think consciousness and cosmology are bizarre beyond human comprehension, you will find your prejudices confirmed in his most recent non-fiction book, *The Weirdness of the World.* He blogs/substacks at The Splintered Mind.

# The Children I Gave You, Oxalaia
## CIRILO LEMOS, TRANSLATED BY THAMIRYS GÊNOVA

One of my oldest memories is of my mother, Maria das Dores, stirring a pot of pinto beans, the kitchen filled with smoke, while I crawled on the packed dirt floor. Good mothers bring me this image. This is how I came to imagine Oxalaia, the Cordylan: a good mother, possessor of a humanity that is my only way to try to understand her.

Oxalaia was stirring a pot of pinto beans when the neighbor from the nest in front poked her round snout through the window and announced that the radio in the yard was playing the voice of an important person. Important human person. Important to Oxalaia was the can on the fire cooking food for the hatchlings, beans more gray than black, hard as river stones, bought on credit from Azpalaz's shop, who had already warned there would be no more credit.

"Do I care about these antics?" she said.

She didn't care; these things weren't for her. In fact, she thought to herself that none of these Earth technologies were for the people of the Cercado. She distrusted things that moved on their own, horseless carriages, contraptions that flew spitting smoke, and radios. Especially radios: voices coming from who knows where, out of boxes attached to poles. They said that down on Ouvidor Street, houses had shell-shaped devices that played music, but in the Cercado, it was a crate high in the yard, for everyone to hear the buzzing of Maxixe and important people from the Control speaking in the Cordylan language, which was just a bit different from the buzzing of Maxixe.

She didn't like the radio, but the hatchlings did. Cosme and Damião didn't come from her eggs, they were human, but she loved them just the same. Did appearances matter? A child was a child, mammal or Cordylan. They weren't twins like the saints of the Terran church, but it was important that they had proper names; Terrans didn't like Cordylan names.

Oxalaia knew that one day the boys would leave to make their lives; it was more than certain, it was inevitable, and they would take the names their mother chose for them. Cosme was two years old and was all belly and head. He was around, playing on the clay floor, looking with his yellow eyes. Damião was four or five and was already wandering the maze of nests as soon as the sun rose, peeking through holes in the cardboard and wooden walls, chasing skinny Venusian chickens, splashing in the mud, or teasing stray dogs.

The hatchlings liked the radio on the pole, not so much for the pianolas dancing chords, but for the group of Cordylans gathering when the Control spoke. The kids laughed and listened without understanding the half-Portuguese, half-Cordylan talk, feeling the salty taste of snot always running from their noses.

The neighbor announced and then left down the alley, drying her hands on her sparse feathers, varicose thighs throbbing. Oxalaia heard the rush through the alleys, saw with the corner of her eye Cosme stand up with a jump and hurry to her side, skinny, long monkey arms raised urgently. He wanted to hear the radio. Oxalaia picked him up and hoped the firewood wouldn't burn too strong and dry out the bean water.

She left with the hatchling hanging. She hated stepping in the mud, but it was impossible to avoid the puddles that took over almost all the alleys, often seeping into the shacks, rotting the wood and cardboard, leaving the outside smelling like crap and the inside smelling like mold. Sometimes, she felt fussy and pretentious for being disgusted by it, while her neighbors, Cordylans like her, sank their feet without caring about the inevitable. Not only did she think herself fussy and pretentious. The others did too. They called her Majestade. This, however, had more to do with her worthless husband than the omnipresent mud of the Cercado, or the fact she spent more of her life on Earth than on the planet of her ancestors. She was a seventeen-heat-cycle washerwoman with two hatchlings of another species living in a refugee favela. Stepping in the mud was the least of her problems, except when she had to step in it.

"Minhão," said Cosme.

"Let's find your brother, my love," Oxalaia replied. She called for the other hatchling, her long fingers shielding her eyes from the sun. The light was pale in most of Rio de Janeiro due to the black clouds vomited by industries. But not on the favela hill. There, it was like gold, taken by the luxuriant green of the vegetation and the dark crust of shanties covering the land like Cordylan feathers. She climbed the alley behind the backstreet, jumped over a sewage line, and went to the embankment where Damião usually played. He was with two other hatchlings, newly hatched, hunting tadpoles in dark puddles between clumps of grass.

"Minhão."

"Come, Damião. Let's listen to the radio in the yard," called Oxalaia. The two little Cordylans pulled their snouts from the water, tadpoles between rows of teeth, cackling with joy. They sniffed the air, stretched their still-short tails, and shot off down the path. Damião, arms as thin as his brother's, climbed the embankment with a huge, very white smile and tried to catch up in the race. A human would always eat dust against a Cordylan, but Damião was still too much of a child to be convinced of his limits. Oxalaia followed behind, dirtying her feet in the mud and hating the hill.

The yard was an empty space between nests and the staircase cut into the clay, a land abandoned by herbs and covered with orange dust. Right in the center, a wooden post, a corpse where sometimes the Control hung real corpses to make clear what happened to Cordylans who crossed the fences. There was a speaker on top that broadcast the National Radiophonic Society's programming six hours a day, twice a week, which included Maxixes, ads from Casa Edison, and odes to Terran rockets sailing the solar system.

Cosme and Damião were already shrugging their little shoulders to the rhythm of Maxixe, and more and more Cordylans were arriving, eyes stretching with curiosity: nest females, unemployed males, tail-stroking rogues, feathered and unfeathered, hatchlings and adults, born in exile or on the planet of their grandparents.

The yard was the amphitheater, the arena, the opera house. Below, Rio de Janeiro, the white buildings, Central do Brasil with its balloon port, and the greenish sea further out.

Filomena (Cordylan name: Veaxiwa), a neighbor, stopped by her side, arm in arm with old Mariano (Cordylan name: Alzpala), her father and father to many.

"What do you think they'll talk about today?" Filomena asked.

"This is Control music. I know because I remember," said Mariano.

"Oh, father, of course it's Control. When isn't it? Could it be good news?"

"If it is, it's not for us," hissed Oxalaia. "It never is."

The sky was full of balloons that day, signaling the route for rockets. "People from Mars," thought Oxalaia.

"Where is Nosso-Rei?"

"His name is Ekundayo, Mr. Mariano. Or better, Manoel, and I've told you countless times we have to use the names they gave us. You talk like that and he takes it all seriously."

"Well, excuse me. But where is he?"

"I don't know about that good-for-nothing," Oxalaia felt the quicksilver running through her veins. Manoel must be at the hill's taverns, drowning in cheap liquor, if there was anyone left willing to give him credit, bragging about his father being a king in the Cordyla jungles before being sold as a slave to the Carnivores' Osmolskae; and that he, rightful monarch, king of all Cordylans refugees on Earth, would one day reclaim his throne and the Osmolskae under his feet and would be grateful to whoever bought him a shot of cachaça.

Manoel was Nosso-Rei, a nickname he proudly bore, oblivious to the malice in the wide mouths that called him that, the contempt for the favela's craziest drunkard, the idle boozehound with delusions of grandeur who didn't starve only thanks to his wife's resourcefulness. Oxalaia hated the nickname, hated the alcoholic king who had replaced the handsome Cordylan she married.

"You're the queen of my nest," he'd say, but she didn't want to be queen of anything, she wanted a marriage according to her grandparents' customs, didn't want to live on the favela, didn't want to have grown up in a world where she was an unwelcome guest, wanted her eggs to come with stronger shells, didn't want to step in the mud, live on pinto beans and flour, so scarce she had to buy on credit from traffickers to avoid starving. Above all, she didn't want to see her husband chased and humiliated by his own people, nor be mockingly called Majestade.

"There he is," Filomena pointed out.

Manoel was floating through the crowd on a cloud of alcohol, all smiles, bristling his blue and yellow plumage, tail swaying. Some Cordylans made mocking bows, and he puffed up and tried to walk straight, distributing greetings and nods.

"My little monkey princes," he said, ruffling Cosme and Damião's hair, then stretching his mouth towards his wife. "And my queen."

The stench of liquor and filth reached her first, but that wasn't why Oxalaia's jaw clenched and her eyes welled up. It was the giggles she heard, the innocent faces of the hatchlings, the Control music on the loudspeaker, the mud drying on her three-toed feet that would get dirty again on the way back to the pinto beans. She turned her face away. Manoel's kiss landed in the void. He took offense at this and became even more irate when he heard one of the subjects say, "Nosso-Rei can't even govern his own female," and the cackling laughter filled the yard.

"I am Ekundayo, the rightful king," he shouted furiously, plumage bristling, teeth bared, tail raised. "King of the Leaf Caste and all the lizards here."

A chorus grew from dozens of mouths, Nosso-Rei-Nosso-Rei-Nosso-Rei, and Manoel smiled, satisfied, proud, full of nobility. Oxalaia wanted to die; didn't her husband understand mockery, was he so drunk or crazy? She dragged her children away.

"I want the radio," Damião whined.

"There's no radio, let's go before the food burns."

"I want to stay."

"Then stay," Oxalaia dropped the older one on the way and stormed through the mud towards the nest, Cosme hanging on her arm like a bundle. Behind her, the chorus of Nosso-Rei faded as the loudspeaker announced, in the Cordylan language, the word of Control.

May was not my favorite time of year. There was something in the increasingly cold air and the newspapers abandoned on the streets full of news about the war against the Cordylans, in the fog that arrived earlier and left later, amplifying my melancholies.

Midnight in a soot-filled city.

I curled up inside the compact universe that was my coat, the wine-colored scarf protecting my nose from the sewer smell coming from the sea. I had just left the National Radiophonic Society, where I wasted my day off from the barracks writing jingles and helping with my uncle Donizete's dubious accounting. In normal times—and by that, I meant eleven and a half months a year—I would close the office doors, receive two condescending pats on the back, buy a bowl of soup to go, take a streetcar home, and waste another two hours with astrophysics books and pamphlets about the solar system, while the soup cooled on the table. But it was May, and there was something strange about May. Nothing worked the same way. I felt quite satisfied with my books and my always-postponed plans for a vacation on Mars, but not in May. Never in May. In May, I wanted to be a Space Hero.

The problem was that almost every Space Hero came from the United States or Germany, even though the launch bases were relatively close, in the Republic of Maranhão. All fighting for the West against the Huns of Titan or the Cordylan guerrillas of Venus. No Brazilians.

I knew I would never travel to these places. But I would settle for more modest orbital flights, and the Farda de Ferro could provide that if I got a promotion.

The opportunity arose when the Control announced he would make a speech to the Cordylan refugees in Rio de Janeiro.

I tried not to tremble beside my uncle and aunt. We were among fifteen people standing on the steps of the Radiophonic Society at 102 Clemente Street, a low, austere building hidden among trees, halfway between the hill and the sea.

The official car parked right in front of us, where Uncle Donizete had a red carpet laid out. The Control got out, escorted by assistants and guards. He extended his hand to my aunt and uncle and greeted them. I expected him to be a small man, full of wrinkles and purplish eyes, wearing a simple but tasteful frock coat, a common man in all respects, not a Germanic giant full of medals and deference. I was a staunch republican. I knew very well that Controls were not kings and looked much more like civil gentlemen than the imposing image in my head. It was 1928, after all. The truth was, despite my rational brain fed by the amateur study of sciences, I was little more than a young man intimidated by teachers, magistrates, officers, and other figures of more or less authority.

The Control insisted on greeting each person before entering the building.

"Today is a great day," he said. He walked through the entrance with another seemingly important person speaking with a foreign accent. My aunt and uncle guided the men, never missing a chance to express how honored they were to receive them.

"Don't leave my side," my uncle whispered to me as everyone settled into the seats in front of the microphones, usually reserved for the small audience invited for presentations. Control drank water and listened to the end of the Casa Edison advertisement (written by me), then the official jingle played. The announcer gave the floor to the Most Excellent Control, his chest puffed with pride, and his tie hanging crooked on his collar.

It was a long, lackluster speech filled with flourishes, simultaneously translated into the Cordylan language. My main concern was not committing the discourtesy of yawning in front of the man, which would surely incur my uncle's wrath. I suspected that Control's ego was as large as the importance of his position. Beneath the starched rhetoric, the performative verbosity, and the self-praise, he announced with great satisfaction to the beautiful Cordylan people that the war was over.

"The armistice has been signed," he said. "Hostilities have ceased. Our Fleet is leaving the vicinity of Venus and heading to a neutral line. The Osmolskae Carnivore guerrilla is willing to accept the Leaf Caste as equals and begin a new era of political fraternity under the United Cordylan Party. All of you can return to your parents' world."

The small audience applauded. I imagined the bilingual speech traveling through the atmosphere and reaching thousands of ears across the country, wondering what the sound of ten million claps would be like and how all of it would sound to the inhabitants of the Cercado.

The official vignette played, a photographer appeared and took some shots for the Official Journal, and, after some generous tips, for Uncle Donizete's private collection. The Control still had a few minutes to answer questions from journalists selected by his press office, such as, "Where would the necessary resources come from to repatriate two thousand Cordylan from the Cercado, besides the thousands scattered across the country?"

Control's answer: the funding would come from partnerships with the private sector and foreign governments, emphasizing that Brazil was the only country with a humanitarian stance to shelter those fleeing the ethnic massacre in the jungles of Cordyla (or, as we know it, Venus), and now other nations were seeking to remedy their embarrassing omission on such an important issue. The real answer: ten million pounds would be borrowed at interest from English banks, using the right to collect port taxes and balloon route taxes for up to twenty years as collateral in case of non-payment. All to send the annoying creatures living in the favela back to the alien jungles where they should never have left and make Rio de Janeiro beautiful and white again.

At the end of the very brief interview, the Control exchanged a few pleasantries with the most important attendees, praised the soft voice of singer Bebel da Glória, the skill of pianist Arduíno de Moura, the distinct diction of announcer Amorim, and the patriotism of Uncle Donizete, who took the opportunity to pull me over and introduce us.

"Who is this young man?" the Control asked.

"He's my nephew, Hilário," Uncle Donizete replied.

"Did he inherit the family voice?"

"I'm afraid not . . . Actually, he serves the country, sir. He's in the Metropol and aims for a spot in the Farda de Ferro."

"I'm sure there are positions for internal service." The Control gave me a good look. "Is that what you want, young man? Know that the National Radiophonic Society provides a great service. You could have a promising future here."

I looked at my uncle. His expression was that of a fisherman whose line had just been bitten, then at the Control, who was putting his hat on and had something mocking in the way he wrinkled his nose and raised an eyebrow.

The Control thought I was a coward. Something boiled inside me. "I don't want to be a secretary, sir. I want to wear the Farda de Ferro suit.

Uncle Donizete was disconcerted by my tone, but the Control smiled and signaled to one of his men.

"Take note of this young man's name. Ask Captain Albornoz to place him in his battalion," he said. He looked at me and added: "I hope you enjoy the experience, young man."

Nosso-Rei was the monarch of the Cercado, the legitimate king of all Cordylans there. In my mind, he walked through the clusters of shacks, navigating the labyrinth of nests like Theseus with his thread, his legs wobbly from the many tiny fingers of the supernatural Brazilian cachaça. There was a map imprinted in his mind, a map as mutable as the fluid structure that surrounded, fed, and consumed him. Dozens of meters above, the clouds parted submissively to the transatlantic airships, whose powerful horns made the zinc, wood, and glass of the nests vibrate. Nosso-Rei didn't care, though. He made his way home, muttering some word to himself, rehearsing the scolding he would give the female who made him pout in front of the entire Cercado. There must be some respect, after all. His father wouldn't tolerate such a thing. Nor would his grandfather, who from his throne of shells would order everyone impaled. Humiliation, even. Especially to him, who even accepted the little monkeys of a female who couldn't even hatch the eggs. But she would see, oh, she would.

He entered the nest, kicking the door to the side. The children were startled. Oxalaia let the pot of beans spill over the wood stove.

"What is wrong with you?" he roared, already staggering towards her.

"You bum, look at the food for your kids on the floor," she despaired, scraping the thin broth with a wooden spoon.

"You embarrassed me in front of the whole Cercado. I'm the king, you can't do that. My respect goes even lower."

"You're not a king, Manoel."

"My father and grandfather were kings, and I am. Ekundayo is my name, not Manoel."

"Look at the beans. What will your kids eat?"

"My kids?"

"Your kids."

Cosme and Damião stood wide-eyed, empty plates in hand, disappointment in their trembling mouths.

"I am from a family of kings!"

"No, you're not!" she shouted, a hatred, a bitterness she had never felt. "You're the king of nothing, you're the worst bum in this dump, you're the king of crap, you tailless lizard, even your kids are ashamed."

His claw exploded on Oxalaia's face. The female hit the opposite wall of the nest, collapsing on the straw bed of the children.

Nosso-Rei immediately regretted it.

"Forgive me, my queen."

"You'll never touch me again," Oxalaia was already on her feet, a small Osmolskae claw hatchet appearing from who knows where. "Never again!" her arm drew an arc in the air, so fast it produced a whistle. She felt the impact on her husband's head through the handle. A spurt of blood. Nosso-Rei fell, screaming, clutching his red-soaked snout.

Cosme and Damião wouldn't stop crying.

"Forgive me, wife," he crawled on the floor trying to hug Oxalaia's legs, crying, begging.

"The beans, look at the beans," she screamed, stomping on her husband's hands, shooing him out the door. He still tried to dig his claws into the doorframe, but he was too drunk. He was pushed into the alley like a bundle of dirty laundry. "Go away! Go! Don't show up here again."

"It's my nest, woman. I'll be back. Oh, I'll be back."

Nosso-Rei was left squealing, watched by the neighbors and two stray dogs brave enough to wander the Cercado.

Oxalaia, shoulders raised, breathing fiercely, feathers on her head ruffled and Osmolskae hatchet bloody in hand, dethroned her king. She was now the mistress of the nest, queen of her own life.

On a Tuesday night, I was doing my rounds, wearing the blue uniform of the Metropol. I wandered around, squeezed between buildings and houses, watching respectable people retreat and the nocturnal fauna take to the streets: drunks, rascals, vendors, people of alternative morals, dockworkers, pickpockets, opium addicts, delivery boys, capoeira fighters, gangs of street children, the idle, the vagrants, the misfits. All watched from above by the Metropol balloon and its searchlights like webs of light.

And I, just another one of the blues.

Or less than one. Don't get me wrong, I appreciated my life and my job. Most of the time. But there was a lack of something, an absence, the impermanence of things, or the permanence of what shouldn't remain, a confusion, a disoriented spinning. In fact, I appreciated my life, except when it was mine and I had to do something with it.

I walked until I felt my feet sinking into the mud and the barbed wire surrounding me. I was at the edge of the Cordylan refugee camp. A dangerous maze, but for some reason, I delved deeper and deeper, a disturbing sense of familiarity.

I needed a guide.

I found it in the form of a Cordylan.

With feathers of colorful and soft patterns, adorned with beads, snake eyes, a long neck, and a sinuous tail. Slightly smaller than me, her vague feminine forms outlined against the entrance of an alley.

"Looking for something?" she said, the Cordylan accent coming softly, a tone reminiscent of bristles of a brush gliding over a rug at the base of the skull. They didn't need to open their jaws to speak with Terrans. The words were a mix of syllables, thoughts, and scents that entered through the ears and nose and bumped into the mind, where they became confused sentences but full of meaning and flavor, as long as the listener was receptive. This made them great poets, and we hated them for it.

"I'm not one of those, ma'am," I replied, looking around to make sure no guard was nearby to see me making unauthorized contact with alien refugees.

"We have a lot to offer. Singing, games, and laments."

Her eyes narrowed, and suddenly there was something there. The taste of fruit wine, the scent of tobacco, the joy of the game, small and ephemeral flashes. All the time in the world.

She didn't cause me the discomfort that the others of her species did, the unpleasant sensation of being near a different race, and at the same time a certain remorse for crowding them into a degrading refugee favela, waiting endlessly to return to their home world. No. There was something almost attractive about that little creature, with her beads, feathers, a dress shaping a bust that didn't exist.

"What kind of laments? Not from lizards, I hope."

"I'm not a lizard, sir," she replied. "I'm from the Leaves, but you know that, I presume. You're not a monkey either."

We called them lizards. Dinosaurs. Geckos. Because that's what they seemed to us. Then, when we learned more and understood the differences, we kept the name, because it insulted and belittled them, and we take great pleasure in insulting and belittling anything.

But Oxalaia seemed much more than a gecko, more than just a mere dinosaur, those lizards full of fear and resentment; she was a piece of incarnate moon, radiating silver rays that slowly penetrated my skin, taking the flesh and perhaps a little bit of the soul, changing my moods to a less bitter stupor. She touched my arm with the certainty of a rain cloud. I allowed it. I felt her scent.

It was like accepting a spell. Now I wanted to follow her into the Cercado, to her nest, to uncover her mysteries, to inhale her vapors, to hear the mellifluous phonemes sliding through me. And she led me, without my noticing anything beyond the desire to be led. She seemed to grow larger, more haughty. Her steps were feline, charged with that insolence that only cats possess. I didn't see the darkness of the alley, the puddles of urine, the snake eyes watching me from the shadows, I only saw Oxalaia.

"All the time in the world," I remember her hissing ten or a hundred times that night, as we drank a fermented liquid and ate a dark mass of beans and wheat, laughing at crude jokes whose meaning I didn't truly understand. The place was a tangle of leaves, fabrics, wood, and cardboard, covered with branches and zinc. Perhaps it was her nest. More Cordylans came sneaking through the cracks, settling around us, singing sad songs under perennial clouds of tobacco, or joyful songs of entwined tails and raising tin mugs, a great ceremony, a ritual, a celebration that lasted hours, years. And I always looked at her, increasingly entrenched behind the warmth of alcohol and aromas, to make sure she was there.

She was.

She danced around two stones the size of melons, came with more drink, more hugs, more singing, more joy, more smells. She touched my wrist with a nail and cut it. A trickle of blood ran from a small cut. I was startled, but she collected the blood with a piece of cloth and used it to draw circular patterns on the stones.

They weren't stones.

They were eggs.

A pounding of cans took over the world, a growing throb, while everyone around me hissed and Oxalaia danced.

She danced a whole world like that. With my blood and my love. When it was over, no egg had cracked. No hatchling born. The Cordylans didn't recreate the world by bringing new life to it. I saw her collapse, nestling in her promises of offspring, her tail almost lifeless, the females around lamenting, turning the celebration of life into a requiem.

One of the Cordylans, with sparse red feathers and bird skulls around his neck, stood before me. I looked deep into his eyes. The powder he blew in my face detached me from the world and dragged me back to the foot of the hill, beyond the barbed wire limits where it was safe for a man to walk.

At the hospital, they said I was intoxicated with lizard pheromones. They're not lizards, I tried to explain. They're Cordylans. But what did all that matter, if Oxalaia had failed to be the mother of the world?

According to the rumors I heard: the Control men came down the alley, knocking from nest to nest. Oxalaia figured it couldn't be a good thing.

"Good day, ma'am," said one of them, tipping his hat. Sweat stained his gray jacket. He had a round face, adorned with the mustache of an important human. At his side, a Metropol officer, a stern and silent young man.

Oxalaia didn't respond to the greeting.

"Would you have some water, ma'am?" asked the mustached one, in Portuguese. A Cordylan posed no danger if it shared its water.

"I don't have any, sir."

"A refreshment?"

"I don't have any, sir."

"This heat is making me jumpy. My gout roars," he smiled, and as the Cordylan remained impassive, he looked to the officer beside him, then to the two small figures that emerged from inside the nest and clung to her skirts.

"What a lovely bunch of kids," he commented. "Are they yours?"

Oxalaia didn't respond. The man realized there was no goodwill there. He wiped his brow with his right arm.

"I'm Olivério Lima, from the Control, and this is Officer Cortes."

"I know what you are," Oxalaia growled.

"The papers are here," Olivério gave two friendly taps on the briefcase he carried. "When you sign, you'll receive compensation for your . . . " he glanced at the front of the nest. " . . . Home. You can go back to your beautiful world with enough to start life over with dignity."

"I won't sign anything. I was born here, I'll die here."

"Ma'am, you need to understand that you're not a Terran citizen just because you were born here."

"I won't sign."

"But your neighbors are signing."

"Then they're all breast suckers," she raised her voice so the nests around could hear exactly what she thought of them. "I won't sign, and I won't sign."

All of Olivério Lima's courtesy drained from his face.

"Ma'am, soon there will be nothing here. Just you and your chicks. Children. The machines will knock everything down. You won't have a home, money, or anything. You'll look at the sky at night and regret not going with your kind back home."

"I hate it here. But Cordyla is worse."

"There's no more war."

"The Osmolskae lie. War will never end."

"The war is over."

"Lies."

"But that's such stubbornness."

"Isn't it?"

"Go back to Venus, Cordyla, whatever you want to call that hole," the officer intervened. "We don't want lizards here."

"I'm not a lizard, and you're no monkey either," she held the Osmolskae hatchet. Olivério cowered behind his briefcase, panting, while Officer Cortes drew his revolver from its holster. Oxalaia saw the barrel pointing right into the gap between her eyes, a dark, menacing, endless tunnel. She imagined the bullet there, a lead shark waiting, eager, to fly into her and shatter her skull.

"Drop it, ma'am," Cortes shouted, holding the gun with both hands, three steps back, scared of his own shadow, with the Cercado looming around him, the gaunt ghosts that could emerge from any hole and take away an arm, a leg. "Drop it in the name of the Control."

"Mother," Damião yelled.

Oxalaia let the hatchet fall, feeling Cosme's little fingers gripping her thighs tightly.

"Please, there's no need for this," Olivério said to the officer. "I would advise you to accept the proposal and sign. You'll end up being forced to do it anyway. But not by us. Goodbye."

Officer Cortes holstered the gun back. He disguised his trembling hands by stuffing them into his pockets and walked out behind the inspector.

"Sorry, sir," he stammered.

"You're an idiot, guard," said Olivério. "You have two thousand lizards in this concentration camp. Pointing a gun here is asking to be lynched. Or does your revolver have two thousand bullets, soldier?"

"No, sir."

"Then calm down. We still have other filthy nests to visit. Besides, that alien has human children with her. That's bound to be a problem. I'll draft a priority report."

"Hardly anyone is signing up. It seems they don't want to go back home."

"And who can blame these wretches? They'll be torn apart there by their old carnivorous enemies as soon as we turn our backs with our fleet." Olivério lowered his voice as they passed by a group of females carrying bundles on their heads and four fiddlers in an alley. "This is just for show. These lizards are leaving anyway."

There was a Cordylan blocking the way. Tall, yellow eyes, a red streak on his face. Feathers and colorful bead necklaces. The inspector and the officer stopped in the middle of the alley: the King of Leaves was blocking their path.

Olivério saw Cortes's nervous hand inching toward the revolver again. He made an impatient gesture for him not to do that.

"Do you gentlemen know who I am?" the Cordylan asked, with a sibilant accent.

"If you could excuse us, sir, we need to join the other twenty armed men who are in these alleys," replied Olivério.

Nosso-Rei opened his arms in a theatrical gesture.

"I'm no thief, gentlemen. Before you stands the True King of Cordyla, Ekundayo."

"Let us pass, Cordylan. It's a warning."

"This is my realm in exile. You step here with your nose up, polished shoes, and bring no gifts. Not even pay homage. And you point a gun in the face of my queen. No one does that anymore. Not here."

Cortes drew his weapon, but an Osmolskae spear severed his hand. He fell without a scream.

"We're the Control agents," the inspector yelled.

"And I'm the King," replied Nosso-Rei. He slit the men's throats with immense joy in his heart.

The Cercado fell silent like a forest when the predator is lurking.

The mass expulsion began at sunrise. It would be a beautiful morning, the autumn light piercing through the natural clouds, white and superior, and the artificial clouds, mean stains sprouted from the chimneys.

The Control inspectors arrived in droves, all alike in somewhat bored expressions and the dull gleam of those who feel wasted in office cubicles, briefcase in hand, cheap suit and hat meticulously positioned, besides the mustache that announced the upright men they were.

The Metropol in blue followed closely behind, solemn watchdogs with furrowed brows, eager to break batons on the backs of enemies of public order.

Office men and barracks men. They knocked on doors, and when the still sleepy Cordylans opened them, the stamped papers and the sight of the golden badge jumped in their faces. In twenty lines, the federal order: pack your things and go live in the middle of nowhere.

The first nests were all rotten, but still obeyed a certain architectural logic, less labyrinthine than the babble of shacks that started in a wall breach and spread like an anthill to the hill. The Cordylans were yanked from their nests and cataloged for repatriation flights.

I was aboard the Metropol armored vehicle. Uncle Donizete's contacts secured me one of the Observer spots, an attempt to scare me. But it didn't. I listened attentively to Captain Albornoz's instructions on the Farda de Ferro's tactics for invasion in case the expropriations became difficult and prepared for the worst.

All I could think, however, was how the Cercado resembled a siren that enchants and then drowns. I remembered being there. I remembered the Cordylan who still appeared in my dreams.

The armored vehicle was quite a machine. The boiler was the largest I had ever seen. The body had a layer of steel capable of withstanding a great deal of damage. Even the hatches and wheels were designed to withstand any difficulty. The gun turrets on the roof were mounted on rails, allowing quick positioning for the machine guns while the gunners sat comfortably inside the cylinders.

It was the lizard killer, the captain joked. He even had scales and a mouth full of sharp teeth painted on the front of the vehicle, covering the old name, *Capitão do Mato*, and renaming it *Tiranossauro*. Resolving conflicts based on the death of the opposing side was the Farda de Ferro's standard, and the *Tiranossauro* was the superlative of all that. It could carry up to twenty men, but only five were there that day: Paranhos, Capistrano, Albornoz, Ferreira, and me. It was a private operation of the Captain's, who wanted to kill as many Cordylans as possible to avenge Officer Cortes, a second cousin. He ordered the men to remove their identification numbers and always keep the skull helmets covering their faces, so the lizards wouldn't identify anyone.

"Not that anyone cares about the talking geckos that kill our people. But just in case, you know. Everyone understood?"

"We understood, sir."

"And you, Observer?"

"I understand, sir."

"Remember to only observe what I command."

"Yes, sir."

"Good boy."

A sliver of sunlight was about to lay down on the puddles of stagnant water. A Cordylan sat atop a pile of garbage and rubble, pondering all that could have been. He was now the wounded king, the prince of uncertainty. The Lord of the Cercado. His Osmolskae-tipped spear was adorned with colorful ribbons and blood.

He squinted and saw a neighbor of his. Walking down the alley, towards him. Others were behind him, footsteps clumsy and uncertain. Two, then ten, then a hundred. More than a hundred. Sprouting from the holes of the Cercado and forming a circle around the throne of garbage. The Cordylan studied their faces. They indicated what was already known: there was nothing but fear. Not a shred of hope or perspective. They needed a leader.

The Cordylan stood up. The sliver of sunlight now shone upon him, giving him a messianic look. He raised the spear.

"They won't send us to death in the jaws of our enemies."

Dozens of eyes gleamed like torches.

"They won't," the Cordylans replied. Your brothers, your weapons. They turned towards the entrance of the alley, where an iron leviathan was climbing up the narrow lane, crushing nests that lay in its path, its painted teeth evoking ancient fears.

The *Tiranossauro* made a maneuver to the left and its flank passed before the trembling Cordylans.

"Cordyla!" shouted the lizard. Could it be Nosso-Rei that I had so imagined? "The Ekundayo that some rumors spoke of?"

The answer came from the artillery. A hail of bullets brought down the saurids closest. The others disappeared into the alleys, while Nosso-Rei ordered them to stay and fight for their homes and their history and their rights. But soon there was no one left besides the *Tiranossauro* climbing the throne of garbage.

Ekundayo raised the spear. The lizard killer shot his arm. With a snap, the Osmolskae spear vanished into the garbage.

The king fell.

"That's what happens to those who kill a Metropol, said the captain, as Nosso-Rei was crushed under the caterpillars of the vehicle.

The smell of beans was a powerful presence inside the nest. It seized everything, driving out the musty odor. Oxalaia liked it. The feeling of comfort. That everything was in its right place. The children, clean and bundled up, delighting in the brown broth, blowing the steam with a hiss and bursting into laughter as tiny specks of saliva flew uncontrollably. The way they said "mom" with their teeth full of bean skins. The bellies plump, full, full. Powerful presence.

But she felt a lump in her throat, a dryness that felt like the air before a downpour. It was dangerous out there. Everyone in the Cercado was edgy and worried ever since that stupid Manoel stuck a piece of iron into the bellies of the Control men. It was a matter of hours, she knew. The earthlings would return those from the Leaves back to the clutches of their killers, while the children would inhabit the sidewalks, with some awning as their roof. Oxalaia looked for the little hatchet. She felt some security in seeing it hanging nearby.

She heard footsteps at the entrance of the nest.

"Your husband is gathering a crowd on the garbage throne," said Filomena, panting.

"I don't want to hear about that scoundrel," Oxalaia replied.

"So be it. An Osmolsake is here. Made of iron. Giant teeth, roars like thunder."

Gunshots convulsed the night of the Cercado.

"The slaughter has begun," whispered Filomena. She cast a last glance at Oxalaia before leaving: "Run, my little one. Run far away and don't look back."

Oxalaia slumped her shoulders.

She went to the wall, picked up her hatchet. Called the little ones. Kneeled for Damião to climb on her back. Tied Cosme to her chest, sheltered in a cloth wrap.

"Hold on tight, ok?"

She ran from there, as fast as she could, fear bringing memories of ancestors running through the plains of Cordyla, when running was the only way not to be devoured by a Carnivore. She stepped in the mud, hating it. But she also realized it was her mud, and familiar hatred was preferable to the unknown.

"Impact," the captain warned. The four of us held onto our seats. The impact, however, was minimal: the *Tiranossauro* went through a barricade of garbage as if it were nothing. "We're in the inner perimeter. Everyone on alert."

The vehicle still went through barrels of water and tore down part of a wooden shack. The pilot turned right and was about to accelerate when Officer Paranhos, looking through the periscope, warned:

"There's someone there."

I felt the smell before seeing the shape behind the smoke and dust. More real than anything around me. As if cobwebs were swept away from an important part of my brain. The doctors had said I was intoxicated with a powerful pheromone, but it wasn't true. There was another kind of connection between us.

There she was, scared, carrying her even more frightened children, facing an armored predator.

"Look at that," the men laughed. "This lizard thinks it's a kangaroo."
Albornoz held the vocal amplifier.

"Put your hands on your head, lizard."

Oxalaia obeyed.

The periscope focused on the face, then moved down the body, the children.

"They're human children. Good Lord," grunted the captain. "Move away from the children now!"

A metallic noise and the cannon moved threateningly.

This time, Oxalaia didn't obey. She jumped over a pile of rubble and ran up the alley, hoping the tangle of nests would make aiming difficult and that the men would take pity and not shoot. She sped up as much as she could, with the children whimpering on her chest and back.

"She's in the crosshairs," Capistrano said.

"But what about the children?" I asked.

"Yeah, the damn kids," Albornoz scratched his chin. "Try to hit her leg. If you hit one of the kids, tough luck. Collateral damage."

I shuddered. For the children and for Oxalaia and for the intoxicating smell.

Capistrano fired only once. The bullet whizzed, cut through the smoke, the cardboard, the stucco, the zinc, and made a groove in the Cordylan's left thigh. She rolled in the mud.

"She fell," said the captain. "Capistrano, Paranhos, go there. Put a bullet in the lizard's neck and bring the kids. Quickly. We've been away from the troop for too long."

The men emerged through the hatch, rifles in hand. I battled something within me. Outside, Oxalaia crawled through the mud that she had always despised in my mind. The captain and the pilot chuckled. To them, it was nothing out of the ordinary. Just another gecko. It should've been the same for me, too. I wasn't supposed to feel the anger, despair, and fear that I felt watching my comrades getting closer to her.

A boiling sensation surged within me, and before I could think of anything, I had my gun pointed at Albornoz's head, shouting to leave my children alone.

My hands trembled, the finger grazing the trigger, the scent of fear cutting through my nostrils like a blade.

"What the hell are you doing?"

"Let them go," I shouted, not recognizing myself. "Now!"

Albornoz hesitated, but I shoved the barrel of the revolver into his mouth and pulled the trigger. He gestured to Ferreira, who seemed as confused as I was.

"Let the dinosaur go," he said through the amplifier. Paranhos and Capistrano stopped, not understanding. "We have a situation here. Come back."

Oxalaia got up and limped out of our sight, her children clinging to her body. It was a long minute, during which they disappeared. Forever.

I released the captain. I threw away the gun, put my hands on my head. He broke my nose with a punch and dragged me out, calling me a traitor. No doubt remained that he would kill me there, thrown in the mud, and I would never see the stars. Or would ensure that I rotted in a military prison for a long time.

But at that moment, I didn't care. I would have done anything for the spell and the scent. Anything for her. For the children I gave you, Oxalaia. The sons I gave you.

Originally published in Brazilian Portuguese in *Dinossauros*,
edited by Gerson Lodi-Ribeiro, 2016

## ABOUT THE AUTHOR

**Cirilo Lemos** was born and raised in Baixada Fluminense, Rio de Janeiro. He helped his father in the woodworking shop and sold hamburgers, ice cream, flowers, and aquarium fish. Today, he is a history teacher, editor, and writer. He enjoys weird dreams, predictable realities, family photos, and Seattle bands from the early 1990s. He currently lives in São Paulo with his wife and has two children who don't know they are clones.

# Those Who Remember the World
## BEN BERMAN GHAN

*"Reason, like information, wants to be free"*
—The Xenofeminist Manifesto

### The Wild Park

The low rumble of the train cut through the night and the living flesh of The City, carrying its passengers ever further from the gleam of parliaments and providence.

The stop towards Wild Park grew ever closer, represented along the wall of the train by a glowing ant that crawled endlessly around the tiny train lines, commanded to chase some invisible prey endlessly up and down, back and forth. When finally, the ant died, other ants would emerge from the firmaments to consume the body and choose a replacement, who would begin the same unmistakable glow and the same symbolic journey along the line: the animal racing towards the end of the tracks—towards the western edge of the world where what sneering mouths of city centers referred to as The Prostitution District lay waiting.

I'll tell you a secret: within the inner city, some don't believe that such a place can exist upon the ever-growing back of the creature that is the world. Why would the vault allow such a place beyond its own strict control? Some mature twist of code must have seen it growing in those early days and declared it a healthy limb of the city, a necessary limb of the city. For what was an urban ecosystem without the mess and the muddle of a multitude of bodily living? Somewhere in the shining sable, an algorithm must believe in the beauty of what its government claims to consider a flaw. Within the rhizomatic structure of The City—a home for the castaways needed to remain—an outer ring of the tree where the elephant shrews feared to tread, turning filth into feature and framework, remaking debris as glorious dressing.

There copulated the artists out of pay, the sex workers in rooms of their own, and the musicians scattered along street corners. Cats cast out from systems of surveillance watch from rooftops with eyes of yellow and green, ignoring the signal that demands they ping reports to the kestrels high above. Why does The City still produce the cats, who have proven themselves incompatible with the circuitry of the systems in which the city's animals must labor?

Nobody knew.

But people grew up there—the only neighborhood in The City where the wild mushrooms grew, and gargantuan Redwood trees burst from between sidewalk cracks, overgrowing ancient urban planning all the way to the banks of the River William, which marked a sharp end to the low buildings—shorelines patrolled by gilled otters who would emerge velvet brown and fangs bared at the first sign of a toe-dipping into the current, determined to keep their waters clean and clear and blue, refusing infestation of mammalian contamination, refusing to allow infections to spread into the life waters of The City.

People like you, who left over and over, your pockets heavy with cargo and the anxiety of being found out. You, who returned in the dark where the train tracks stopped. When the train settled into its place to sleep in the deep of the night, its ants curling into death, you emerged in song—the ancient odes to American Idiots that were long ago stored in the vault but cannot be understood, humming absentmindedly from between your lips. Sure, the lyrics make no sense to you. But you have that gift of language given to children of The City. You can infer. The gold rim of your glasses caught the light as you climbed up the steps into the fresh wet air, and your foraging pouch swung from an awkward clip along your belt like a black, swollen moon.

The song died in your throat when you entered the light of the street, and found the otters of the districts on their hind legs, their black coats glittering in the streetlights, looking up at the boy no older than you, suspended from the low branches of a baby redwood tree. Arms and legs splayed and pierced outwards so as better to see the complicated disaster of his opened body. The punctures were twofold in the shape of a starfish, once across the torso, once across the throat as if in microscopic recreation of the larger violation.

There among the fungi, you scrambled to help him, to set him down against the soft base of the tree, and as you did, the otters scatters, fleeing back to the rush and roar of their aquatic zone. From terrible bite marks, his blood flowed rich and deep, a cellular mix of fleshy liquid fauna held so long within his bodily container.

You called his name. But all he did was stare upwards, stare past you as the smell of food and firewood signified the streets of your home tinged with the horrible scent of rot.

What do you think he saw, up in the midnight sky, that made his dark eyes go so wide? Cracked lips parted. His voice was a gurgle through the night.

"I'm not alone," he said.

"No," your voice, shaky but clear, as you hold him as if trying to hold his horrible wounds closed. "It's me. It's Mina. I'm here."

"I'm not alone," he echoed. But he didn't mean you. His sticky fingers found their way to the open throat, to the horrible nightmare of his own body. He bled, and already armies of microscopic sporous fungi were racing into him; mycelial forces lay claim to the precious micronutrients within the meat. They were an eternal dominion of constantly expanding life, the delight of the matter of the dead. "I remember," he said.

"Remember what?" you asked. You wondered when someone would come and find the two of you, when an adult might step around the corner and stand you up and brush you off and this violent reality.

He clutched at you, wet fingers smudging the red text of your shirt. He whispered something to you, something the ever-watchful cats could not hear. Then his arms dropped, and his breathing stopped. Within the horrible starfish cavern of his stomach and throat, baby mushrooms were already thriving.

### This is a public service announcement:

November 13th, 8453

Please note that the moratorium on mushroom picking in the Wild Park District remains indefinite. Trading unregistered fungi in commercial and private settings remains illegal; failure to comply with City Commerce Regulations will result in strict penalization.

Additional memorandum:

December 11th, 8453

An animal malfunction has been reported; several civilians have been reported missing. Please avoid prolonged exposure to The William.

Residents north of Ironwood & Railway should be considered warned of potential risks after nightfall. Consider this warning to remain in effect until an update can be issued. An Investigator has been dispatched to the neighborhood courtesy of the Parliament of Containment.

Emergency services will not be dispatched in case of injury or fatality

Co-Signed:
   *Representative A:* The Parliament of Commerce
   *Representative T:* The Parliament of Agriculture


"Do you take?"

The little capsule in my hand, outstretched, no larger than a dime. Ruby red. You shook your head, doing your best not to look at it, or my hand, or me.

I shrugged, I withdrew. Placing the capsule between my teeth—biting hard, feeling it dissolve into vapor's that curl out from my nostrils and between my lips.

"I thought caps weren't allowed anymore," you said. It was the first thing you'd said to me, the first victory, small, important, essential. "Containment rounded up all our vendors."

"I'm already of containment," I said. "I'm already contained." It was true. A steady diet of low-grade hallucinogens was a healthy and necessary vice, allowed even by the city that disavowed it. A tiny mercy. "You'd prefer the mushroom cakes, I suppose," I said. I smiled through my smoke, feeling the acid hit my bloodstream and demanding my nervous system make all the colors of the room just a little warmer.

"I've never had the mushrooms," you said.

"Then, of all the folks around, you are exceptional." My laughter was short and grating, the sound of wet rasping things. When I heard it, I stopped. I didn't think I'd ever heard my own laugh before.

You were staring at me. Nobody had told you yet that your glasses were ever so slightly askew. Nobody had yet offered a change of clothes, and against the black stomach of your shirt, the dark brown stain of a handprint. Did blood always dry to brown in such fabrics?

I did my best to settle. The room they'd given me for interviews was unnamed and unused. Black metal piping lined the walls, and a window placed the dark in the northwest corner of the room, allowing a small and careful invasion of light, light eating at the vapors that curled out of my nostrils, mingling with notes of dust. "Can you tell me why you were coming out of the Wild Park Station so long after curfew?"

"One of my mothers at Clementine. She likes to sew."

"I see."

"She makes the quilts."

"I see."

"She asked for materials. From the inner city. There are dyes and fabrics in Paper Town we don't have out here."

"Yes," I said, agreeable, confirmable. "But so late after curfew."

"Nobody follows the curfew," you said carelessly and easily as if I weren't the agent of Containment sitting on the other side of the little iron table across from you. It was as if Commerce, Knowledge, and Application did not stand behind me.

"Nobody?" I asked before biting my tongue, feeling the blood, angry about my easy admission of ignorance. "What did he say to you?" I asked, moving on from the stumble, narrowing in, focusing. But focus was hard. In your gaze, I had found an unsettlement and an amber, a light, a little hint of daytime leaking through, like the light from the window, infecting the room, infecting me.

"He told me he remembered the world," you said as if you were doing as much to steady yourself as I was.

"What do you think he meant by that?"

"I don't know," you said. You breathed out. A long sigh, the scent tickling my nose. Honey and sandalwood and something else, hidden, earthy, rotting. "Do you?"

"Do I what?"

"Do you remember the world?"

The words were in the air. I breathed in. They were in my lungs. I could feel them, creeping, the sonics of your voice, echoing inside the empty chambers of my body, whispering: *the world the world the world.*

For a long time, you stared at me. Neither of us said anything. You studied my face, and so I did my best impression of a mask, of something impassive, something as cool and cold as the black metal of the room. What were you looking for in my creases? In my asymmetry? I didn't like it. The way you studied and assessed. I needed a way to make it stop.

"Before we continue," I said, probing, breaking the silence, "Maybe this is yours?" from the folds of my jacket, I took out a silver wristwatch, it's glass face cracked, it's screen dead. I turned it over to show the initials *M.C.* Engrained on the back

You started, reached forwards, and then stopped, your fingers inches away. "Where did you find this?" you asked.

"On the body."

"I didn't know he had it," you murmured, staring down at the little thing. I suddenly felt very stupid, holding it out to you the way I was. I set it down on the table between us. You looked back up at me sharply. "But isn't this like, evidence?" you asked, "Are you allowed to just take things?" I didn't say anything. I felt myself flushing—this hadn't even occurred to me. "Oh god," you said, so quiet that ears less sharp than mine might not have heard. "Oh, mothers. Oh god."

"What?" I asked.

"No, I'm sorry, it's just. You're so new, aren't you? You're so young."

I should have known then who you really were. I should have known where you would take me if I agreed to follow.

Yes, I was new compared to you.

Four years. Out of the black, into the dark. Four years of only nights. That's how long since I was decanted, since I was molded, spliced, surgically placed within the meat of things. I fell into dreams when the sun came up, for somewhere in my design was the element of the bat or some other nocturnal animal.

What have I been doing for four years? The city is an organism, organized, orderly. Perfect. The city is alive, the circuitry of its vault running through all structures, all streets. The city is an animal, forever telling on itself. A single mind. A more perfect machine.

So, what does a place with no secrets from itself need from an investigator? That was the question I asked of the machines that wiped the amniotic fluid from my eyes as my consciousness burst like a trillion lights throughout this strange flesh I find myself of.

I was a creature of questions. I was a creator of containment. That is what the humming ghost of the vault—the city's secret god, had told me.

And then it pushed me out, a splinter dropping from the wound. The AI god of the city is an honest god. For four years, I was contained. Waiting. Wondering why.

Then I heard it. Beautiful. Perfect. Unknown. I heard screaming. I heard you screaming. I heard the body drop from the trees. I heard the Killer thing, and I heard the god of the city ask a question.

*What was that?* god asked. *What's happened?*

I would be the animal that answered, that delivered, that contained. I would give god an answer.

After the interview, I dove into history, into you. I swam through the long, genetic soup of the Vault's memories, of every report of the birds, that stream back into the black tower.

You came not from The Vault's cold and pristine centers, designed and ordained with purpose. Cold hands of complicated fiber optics didn't pull you from growing vats, shaking nutrient slime from your already grown body.

Instead, the soft and clever fingers of Koala nursemaids pulled you wet and red-faced and screaming from the body of a mother, blood, and fluid staining sheets in the only room of the Clementine Co-op that could be considered sanitary enough to serve as a Delivery room—though throughout Wild Park, sanitation was often a term of compromise.

Without the strict regulations of the City's watchful eye, contamination was inevitable. For many, that was a joyous thing. Intermingling was inevitable. Cohabitation between companions, external and internal, was the driving and thriving force of the community.

But exposure remained a danger. For your mother, still so exposed and so ravaged by a difficult pregnancy, and for the tiny body inspected by marsupial fingers: you. Such a little creature, not quite able to see, knowing nothing but sensation and the sharp, sudden violence of being. You, with flesh so thin it could not keep out the world, with its traces of animal and fungal invasion.

You were taken from the room by warm hands not because you were not wanted but because the children in Clementine were raised communally, and another was waiting with the care and milk you needed while the birth mother who spilled you forth recovered.

The unknown Thing, the killer Thing, had not arrived in the forest edges of your neighborhood then. It couldn't be found in the cracks of the dusty bricks of Clementine, the fountains of happy buskers and loiterers of the arcade, or the thick, dark rush of the river. But it was coming.

*Do you remember the world?* Your words. His words. Someone else's words. Burrowing into me, like the opening of a riddle or the first verse of a poem. A contaminant of language, inside you and inside me.

Inside the body splayed out before me on the examination table, the dual starfish-shaped wounds were already riddled with fungi and rot. The closer I came to the corpse, the more your words seemed to worm around in my memory: a signal yearning to be free.

I cracked capsules and blew my smoke, staring down into the ruined body—the mystery of the victim. He lay on a cold steel table in a white room. Outside, a thick fog rolled, and bumblebees danced playfully along the ledges of the parliament. There, far from you and Clementine and Wild Park and the ever-churning river, the investigation turned physical in the Parliament of Containment, where the only faces that were not metal were my own. Between me and the body, me and the mystery, the autopsy bot moved in complicated gestures, its body humanoid only in the vaguest shape, comprised of many connected concentric circles—orbs which contained the tools to cut.

"We appreciate your dedication to the work, Lucy, but we want to reiterate that your presence at this time is not strictly necessary. Any relevant findings will be made available to you." God's voice came from no specific circle but from the body as a whole.

"I'm The Investigator," I said. The bot hummed God's acknowledgment and began its work.

"Victim is twenty-two years of age, natural born. Citizen residency D.10111610UC."

"His name was Destan," I said.

There was a momentary pause as circles upon circles hovered over the body. "Yes, thank you, Lucy," God said.

"*Investigator*," I repeated. The vapors from my capsule vanished into vents that sealed like gills along the side of the walls. Without that soothing burst of sensation, I could feel an itching in my skin, like a thing made of words pushing at me from the inside. I could see your face painted inside my eyelids. I could see your fear, your confusion. I could hear the words upon your lips, against my lips. *the world, the world.*

"Please note that injury on right hand is to be excluded from further investigation."

"Why?" I asked.

"It does not bear the markers of the other wounds inflicted. Early judgments would say it is from at least thirty minutes prior to attack. The victim . . . simply cut his hand on something. Size and shape of wound indicate perhaps a kitchen knife. When we turn to the primary wounds along torso and throat, we can see that fungal growths around the edges of the incisions have slowed from the initial rate of infection to a state of dormancy unusual for such species. Hypothesis: awaiting signal?"

"Signal?" I asked. A sweet yet rancid smell filled the air as if something like sugar had been set on fire upon the table.

"During the early construction of the city, with the majority of biolife still in development, sporous networks were deployed to allow better communication between The Vault and the host body, which is the world."

*The world, the world.*

A pause. The circles turned in place. The autopsy bot had no eyes, yet still I could feel the god of the vault looking at me. "Are you alright, Lucy?"

"Investigator," I snapped.

"Investigator," conceded the voice. Are you alright?" I nodded. The circles returned to their task. "Secondary hypothesis: the growths are merely byproducts—meant to disguise the theft of genetic material."

I stepped forward until the corpse came into sharp focus, past the form of the machine. "There is something," I said. The smell was growing stronger on the table, that stinking burning sugar. But beneath the rot was more, a flicker—a movement. I looked down at Destan, and he looked back at me. As my eyes moved, his eye moved, tracing me, tracking me.

I pointed. The eye focused on the tip of my finger. A single circle opened at the end of the bot's long arm. The knife was exact, was tiny. "Excuse us, Investigator," it said. "Please note the time and nature of the incision. One millimeter cut only."

Knife into jelly. A gentle *hiss* like air escaping hollow space. No blood or leaking human gunk made itself known. Instead, the eye, like an eggshell, cracked and crumbled. From that hollow space, the movement continued. I leaned forward because I couldn't help it because I couldn't resist it. In the socket of the eye of the dead, a microscopic, little salamander blinked up at me, two eyes of its own like pinpricks that stood out among black spots on red skin. Then a second appeared, then a third. A litter of bright red salamanders the size of colony ants, writhing and blinking out at me. "The world!" It cried out, voice horrible and strange, plucking the words from inside my head and throwing them back to me, distorted and strange.

"What the fuck?" I said.

Upon my voice, the many tiny amphibians snapped to attention, their mouths opening wide. "Investigator, I think perhaps you should recuse yourself," said the machine.

"*THE HOUSE OF THE WORLD!*" shrieked the salamanders, tiny voices mingling and overlapping and warping. Then the body exploded. From each pour, red emerged, wriggling and screaming and scrambling toward me. They filled the room like sand within seconds, replicating, duplicating, and expanding outwards and outwards with ever more minuscule limbs and eyes and gripping fingers.

I could feel them beneath my clothes, pressing to my skin, their soft, cool hands adhering to me, pushing into me, seeking new homes in my flesh. Perhaps the voice of god still spoke to me, still cried out in alarm, as the salamanders welled up around my throat, pushing at my lips, diving into my ears, tumbling down my throat, snouts pushing at the corners of my eyes seeking entry.

But I couldn't hear God anymore. I could only hear the animals as their bodies filled my body, and their incantation swarmed within my flesh, consumed my organs, stuffed my veins fat and full with scales. Then everything turned to black and the sweet stink of burning sugar—and all that remained were the salamander's words, your words, drowning me from the inside with the many bodies of your voice.

*Standing in the shadow of the house of the world was a garden and the garden was time and its soil was the dead and the yet to be and we took our tools and we pulled up the roots and stone foundations and as the house of the world of shadows crumbled before us we took our soil and took our flowers and trees and fungal spires and stole it and caged it and ran with it and we were inside the cage and inside it until there was no world and no house but only the garden and its worms and writhing limbs and rot which filled our mouths as outside the cage we ran and so the many handed corpse of the garden made home inside you and inside me and inside the cage of the garden of time we could only remain the animals that remembered being dead and only when we leave the garden will we remember the world but the world needs nothing to remember us and the world remembers us for we are standing in the shadow of the house of the world was a city and the city was time its buildings were the bodies of the dead and yet to be and we took our tools and we dismantled the city . . .*

In the aftermath of the autopsy, I hung suspended in a quarantine self-imposed, while a hundred agents of Containment carrying the voice of God told me over and over again that I was clean, that the infestation had been incinerated, that no trace of amphibious bodies inside my flesh no matter what I felt, what I saw, what I heard.

There in the small room where I had spent the first years of my life waiting for that first call, that first investigation, I came unfurled. Out of shoes, by long curved toes found purchase on the ceiling, and many species of bat that swirled within my genomes found satisfaction as the blood rushed to my temples. I hung that way, eye level with the one sliver of window that was my gateway to The City.

In one direction, I could see the distant twinkling lights of Wild Park, where *you* waited, with the mystery and the lurking thing that had killed and placed its screaming words and squirming red bodies within the flesh of the dead.

And there, in the exact opposite direction, spiraling outward from the center of the city, I saw the Vault, stretching upwards, filling the air with its walls of darkened crystal.

Whatever had killed the boy in Wild Park had not so with random violence but a design, an intention against the intentions of perfect order that was The City and The Vault itself. What would work against a vault? In my head, among the curling words of the salamanders, a shape had formed. In my mind's eye, I saw you standing in the city with your back to that black and glittering tower of thought. You were not looking up but looking down. Not to a tower, but a pit. Not a vault, but an expanse, a descent. Something bright and shining and burrowing deep into the open bleeding flesh of The World.

Elephant shrews settled in their darkened nests along the underpasses of the city, tiny shivering bodies hiding from the heavy rain that covered our metropolis, a storm to slaughter a generation of beetles in the flood. In Wild Park, the Otters of the William did their work endlessly and tireless.

High above the dark and furious clouds, nothing moved, nothing danced, and nothing save for the Otters bore witness to the Denizens of Wild Park as they gathered by the banks of the William, where the streets of their neighborhood came to a sharp and sudden end. They stood arms outstretched, illuminating the night with the dancing glow of jarred fireflies, grief-stricken faces turning to me as I walked through them, bodies parting for me as if some deep animal instinct understood and responded to the emanations of my body that sang *I am not one of you*, the ancient song that the bodies of predators had always sent through the civilizations of prey.

The second victim, the second body, hung suspended and opened from strange white fungi that seemed to blossom from inside their wounds and root themselves downward into the earth, the double starfish patterns along their throat and torso identical to what we had seen before. Though unlike the first, nobody had found this body while she still clung to life. Nobody had been there to be infected by the words flowing into the world with their blood.

Instead, the message was carved in glowing blue, fire upon the banks of the William that the rain could not extinguish. I didn't bother to look away from them. I didn't bother trying not to read. I saw no point in trying to hide it from the onlookers. It was too late for that. I no longer felt the urgency of containment or the vicious stinging threat of contamination. I was past contamination. Beyond contamination.

*THE WORLD REMEMBERS US.*

Behind me, a scuffling, a murmur. I could feel you trying to push your way through the crowd of bodies that had given way to me with such ease. I could hear recognition sparking, conflict brewing into voices, yours and others, blending together in a breathless chant: *oh Mina, honey, please don't look/let me through/Mina no you don't want to see/please let me through!/Mina come here/Mina come back/baby no/ girl no/Mina no . . .*

And then you were beside me, and we gazed together and the fire and the writing your mother had left behind before her body was transformed by horror. I knew it was her before you were beside me. For in that ruinous frame, the eyes had remained intact and open, though I thought, perhaps, tiny red bodies within the skull were already beginning to move inside the jelly. But all the same, those eyes were the same as yours.

There would be no further excavations for the dead of the Wild Park. When the rain cleared, the body was burned in hot and hungry fire. Nothing was left behind but ashes to fall into the river—gobbled up by the hungry otters. No possibility of escape for whatever wriggling bodies had hidden away within the rotting flesh.

"My friend, my parent. And you. The way you look at me." I tried so hard not to look at you. "What am I in all this?" You asked.

We sat together upon the roof of the Clementine Co-Op, where you had lived most of your lives, our feet dangling from scaffolding. To our backs, unions of meerkats with serious mouths worked their way through the vegetation, tending the bushels of cherry tomatoes and sweet fruits that had been almost drowned in the storm.

"I don't know," I said.

"But you knew there was something about me."

"Yes."

"You didn't see me as a bystander or a witness."

I felt wriggling beneath the skin of my hands, some tiny bodies trying to break free that might answer you better. "A witness," I said.

"What do you see when you look at me?" You asked. I shrugged. I stared at the rooftops. "Look at me."

I did. Your eyes, so like the dead. The furious curve of your frown. Your grief is heavy upon your cheeks. I saw the pit leading down into the world. I saw something climbing out of it, climbing towards you— an idea placed inside my head by the bodies that had climbed inside my body. "I see something circling you," I said. "Something acting in discord with the world."

I fished another capsule from my pocket, made to bring it to my lips, but you stopped me, your hand on my wrist.

"Nobody I'd known had ever died before," you said, and little tears clinging to the roundness of your cheeks. You were sitting so close to me, your shoulder brushing against mine, and some animal part of me yearned to reach out and bite it. "How did you know it was coming for me?"

How *did* I know? Why had my attentions landed on you, and only you, before all others, the moment I had seen you? I caught myself then, staring at you the way I hadn't realized I was always staring at you. You looked back with those black eyes I could never quite read. I watched the pulse beating in your neck. I watched the black hair that clung to your pursed lips. A flush crept up my chest, a burning heat that pushed the salamanders beneath my skin out of the way until even my cheeks warmed. I stared at you, my eyes wide. My mouth opened. Words didn't come.

"Ah," you said. "I see," and your words were fangs sinking into me. "You really are so young."

"I don't . . . " I started, with nowhere to take the words. And then you kissed me, your mouth rough and wet against mine, and that sickly burning sweetness that had remained against my tongue was vanquished, and I breathed you in, in scents of buttercream and earthy dampness, as if I were lying along a wet and mossy river, where mushroom caps might freely blossom. Inside me, the many tiny bodies hum, their endless chant almost finding rhythm, and with powerful certainty, I know this contact between us makes them *happy*.

I push you away. It hurts like aching rivers inside me. Your smile is bitter and sad and unsurprised. "Maybe you'll get over it," you said.

But I knew I wouldn't.

### Missing Persons

We were in this together now, you and me. People had died in your home. I was not enough. What was it about you, beyond instinct, beyond attraction, that had brought such violence to Wild Park? What was this thing stalking you, eating away people whom you've touched, and laying its terrible screaming envoys within their flesh? Seven days between the first death and the second. Six days to go before another. This was my first case. You were my first partner.

"How do we know Destan was first?" You asked.

"No prior bodies have been found," I said.

"What about bodies that haven't been found?" You asked. "Do people ever go missing in The City?"

My first case. My first partner. You asked the questions I was too young to ask.

People walk through the city and think of themselves as unseen, individuals among millions, unimportant and unrecognized and unwatched—so long as they tuck the brims of their hats down low and do not make eye contact with the hummingbirds and kestrels and fancy floating invertebrates. They forget what The City truly is, what *The World* truly is. It doesn't matter who or what sees or does not see you. There's no hiding from an animal when you are crawling across its flesh.

People *think* people go missing all the time. People change their name, people move, people go into hiding. They hide from other people, maybe. But not from the city. Very, very few people *actually* go missing.

So we sat together in your little apartment in Clementine, and I closed my eyes and called forth the God of the vault, and one named glowed among the others—one cross listing, with a history of contact with you, pre-dating the first Wild Park Killing.

**Requisition Request 001:**
**List of Missing Persons Reports November 8452-November 8453**

Delivered at the request of The Parliament of Containment.
- Destan Clementine (Deceased)
- **Zhorah Pedicab NX-1702**
- Hazel Rice (Detained)
- Francesca Crow (Recovered)

"About a year ago, an office from the Parliament of Culture reached out—the usual ways. People in the City's core districts like to pretend it never happens, even though they call Wild Park *The Prostitution District.* How do they think that would work if they didn't seek services? They think we sell ourselves to ourselves, to support ourselves?"

"And you went."

You shrugged. "It was Destan's usual contract, but he was on a foraging hunt. It was a good contract, it wasn't special. It took me out to Paper Town. The offer promised anonymity and payment."

"But The City always knows," I said.

"I guess it does," you said.

"And you met them there? Zhorah Pedicab NX-1702?"

"They just called themselves Zee."

"Zee," I said. I closed my eyes. There was an ache in the base of my neck. It had been there since the autopsy, tugging at me. "Do you think, if I took you to Paper Town, you could find your way back to where you met them again?

## Senator

Across the burning purple sky, birds were flying northward, returning to the silent maw of The Vault. Among them flew a Fish, carrying us safely inside the caverns of its belly.

Your face was pale. You chewed the inside of your lip; your fingernails dug into the mossy edges of your seat.

"Not much longer," I promised, tongue like sandpaper on the roof of my mouth. A curt nod without looking at me. Beads of sweat upon your temple. "This is your first fish?"

"The trains are better," you said.

"The trains are slower," I said, "But they can't smell contraband, can they?" You gave me a sharp look, but I only smiled. "It's alright," I said. "This Fish is assigned to me, so nobody tracks it as carefully. I thought it might be better for you not to have any record of leaving the community with a representative from the Parliaments." My hands moved in small gestures that said I didn't care if you sold mushrooms to the inner city even though, as a creature of containment, it should have been my job to care about such things.

The fish lunged forwards, down towards the streets of The City, and within its belly, the turbulence shook us.

*Only when we leave the garden will we remember the world.*

"Do you think we're helping, leaving Wild Park right now?" You asked, and it occurred to me how rarely you must have left the streets of your youth. "Are we doing the right thing?"

I looked straight ahead. From the corner of my eye, I could feel something writhing beneath my fingernails, could feel tiny bodies trying to push themselves out from my forefingers. A single red body, tail twitching, tongue lolling over piercing golden eyes to clean them of blood and dirt and goo, crawled out from my finger, scampered down my pant leg and vanished into the belly of the fish. I gave it no reaction. You gave no indication you had noticed it at all. "Yes," I said. "I think we are doing the right thing."

*Only when we leave the city will we remember the world*, rumbled the voice in my head, growing slowly stronger.

We disembarked in the dark at dusk and emerged into Paper Town's sleepy streets at the corner of Candlefish and Library. The air was thick, wet, and hot, and from the moment it touched, I could feel my shirt clinging to my back, forming damp spots—the promise of oncoming storms.

Across the square, The Senator Hotel sat embedded among rows of Weeping Fig Trees, a long building of pale stone whose windows glowed a soft inviting yellow. My eyes strained upwards to the sixth of seven floors, to the one red-framed window whose lights were out.

Scowls of annoyed disinterest melted into guarded curiosity as the manager recognized the colors of Containment in the hem of my coat as we entered the lobby. He gazed at us through thick cataracts, guided forwards by the black lemur that hung from his shoulder. In silence, the three of us ascended in the glass elevator overlooking the lobby.

We stood before a door, old wood painted white, chipping from neglect. *Pedicab Room* was still stick to the door with a little plaque, under the room number, signifying a more permanent occupancy over the more causal short term stays that the rest of the hotel served.

"Why haven't you cleared out the room?" I asked the manager

The lemur tugged on his arm, pulling at his attention. The manager shrugged. "They're still paying," he said.

"But their . . . " you hesitated, glanced at me. "They're not around, anymore."

The lemur chittered, angered by questions. I took a step forwards and it scuttled back, hiding behind it's companions thin legs. "Someone's still paying," the old man said. I nodded, and man and monkey wandered away, making their way back to their eternal placement behind the desk in the front lobby.

Before we went in, I held the handle, and asked you to describe what you remembered.

"A little small," you said. "A little messy. All the furniture squeezed in. Burned coffee on the stove."

"What do you remember of them?" I asked.

"Vacant," you said. "Bored, maybe. Nobody really home. Just a worker. Nothing special."

In the dark, scent came first, but scent could be enough. I was made to make my way through the dark.

The stink of abandonment. Of rot, and wet. Of mold, and ancient used coffee grinds. But beneath it, behind it. That other smell. The one that had been following me. The sweetness the dead carried. Sugar and smoke, like candy in a fire.

Behind me, I heard you choking as you tried to step through the door frame. Your hand covering your nose and mouth, eyes wide trying to find the light.

"He left in a hurry," I said. "No tidying up. No packing. But it's all wrong. The coffee is too fresh. Someone came here, after Zhorah's missing person report was filed. Maybe only by a few months, but still."

You didn't question my olfactory sense. It did nothing for me to hide them. Agents of parliaments were bred, it wasn't a secret.

The light hummed on.

It wasn't a large suite. A bachelor, cramped kitchen, with year old dishes still waiting to be pulled out of the sink. A mocha pot knocked over from the counter, making old stains upon the wood of the floor. By the window, a green velvet chaise lounge was stained with a long streak of coppery brown. Old blood, or something strange. Old papers, torn out of a notebook or ledger, were scattered everywhere. All along the walls, the floors, scratch marks like notches, in pairs of three or five, chipping the wood, leaving little streaks of that same coppery brown.

"Oh god," you said. "They were attacked."

"No," I said. "No sounds of struggle reported. No markings by any second set of hands."

You remained close to the doorway, as if you could escape the smell or echoes of violence, as if some artificial boundary could keep it all away from you. In the corner next to the bed, a closet door was ajar. Around it, the markings changing. But I didn't need to see that to know I had to open it. I didn't need to make out the twin starfish patterns in the wood. All I needed was that smell of fire and sugar, that grew ever stronger.

Even as I wrapped my hand around the door handle, I knew what I would find. I could feel tiny hands and feet and tails squirming in my stomach, racing down the bones of my arm. There, written on the inside door, in that same rust brown, sweet and burning: *I Remember Being Dead.* I turned away, doing my best to see and not to see, to take in the words without them. I leaned down, plucked one of the little pieces of paper from the ground and turned it over: *I remember the world.*

I knew how it would go on from there. Knew how the words would change and warp along each sheet of paper, on windowsills, on the underside of the sofa, beneath the bed, until they became the chant that hummed and throbbed inside me, until they became *Standing in the shadow of the house of the world was a garden and the garden was time.*

"You think they did this to themselves?" You asked, horrified.

I squeezed my fists tight. Salamanders would not escape my flesh. "Everybody does," I said.

Out the window in the early morning, an otter was making its way down the street, so far from the rush of the it's river home, lumbering and black. It turned its head, as if to stare up at me. I see the small red of its lips

"The manager said the rent is still being paid," you said, as I watched the sleek creature turn the corner, disappearing into the sleeping intersection.

"He did, yes." I turned back to you. We stood a little closer to each other, as if nearness might protect against the violence of the room. You took my hand. I let you, even though I felt the tremor running through me, even though I felt the words curling inside my flesh.

"Do we have any idea who that might be?" You asked.

## A Place of Culture

In the empty dark of the galleries of the parliament of culture, a woman spilled her tea, sending chamomile and spattering across the white marble floors. The little teaspoon rattled away into some unknown crevice, the white porcelain teacup shattered, a tableau of many little pieces. From the quiet corners of the parliament, urgent spiders began to spool downwards towards the mess. "Please don't," she called to them, sliding her mirrored sunglasses into a breast pocket, revealing pink and complicated compound eyes. "It's fine. I can do it."

The arachnids retreating, their many limbs twitching in disappointed, bodies shivering in a longing to be of service. She knelt there on the floor, unbothered by the wet splashes of tea that stained the knees of her cream colored linen suit, slowly gathering tiny little shards to drop into the palm of her hand.

"Lean times for culture?"

She flinched, but held it close, swallowed it, continued to peer towards the many little fragments of the broken teacup still all around her—a true professional. "We are a city of industry and knowledge and change. Culture always has a place in things."

A woman in coats of long grays and black stepped forward as if melting out of the shadows, a face gaunt, whose black eyes glittered and whose dark hair was pulled back in braids to reveal ears ending in sharp, curved tips. The brush of fabric and the *click* of shoes in the motion of kneeling down. The crooked smile revealing canines to long and pointed for the mouth they nestled in. I didn't think about my appearance that much. Growing up inside the walls of Containment, peering out of thin windows towards the lights of the city, there never seemed much space for reflections. It was enough to give even the Minister for Culture a moment of pause. "You are Minister Minerva Culture NC-1701?"

"Are you here representing Change?" She asked, and my peculiar ears could interpret the melodies of hope and fear behind those words.

"I represent Containment," I said, though that felt wrong then, felt as untrue as saying I was here from The Vault. Increasingly, inevitably, I represented *you*. It occurred to me then, seeing myself in the strange eyes of Culture, just how peculiar the way you looked at me truly was. I knew that Culture saw a bat, huge and malevolent crouching towards them. But when you looked at me, you saw only me.

She tilted her head, mantis eyes studying me. "What does Containment want with Culture?"

"It's not about the parliaments or anything like that." There you were, walking out from behind me, as if you, like me, had been bred to become enveloped by the dark. A true partner in the craft I'd been made for, an investigator all your own. "We just want to ask if you know what happened to your brother."

## Requisition Request: 002

Flagged Signature: Communication from The Parliament of Culture to The Parliament of Knowledge. Delivered at the request of The Parliament of Containment.

*Simon,*

*My office thanks you for the endorsement following the Summit at Sunshine, and I hope this can be the beginning of a long and strong relationship between Culture, Knowledge, and Change. Please acknowledge that the terms of our arrangement has been kept, and note that this is not a permanent exchange. I remain in waiting for confirmation of Zhora's cooperation and safety.*

*Warmly,*
*Representative Minerva Gi NX 1701*
Dated October 18, 8452

## Requisition Request 003:

*Simon,*

*It has been nearly twelve weeks since the agreed upon exchange. I have not been updated as to my brother's whereabouts, his mental or his physical status. I understand these things take time, but the exposure to Change, as it was explained to me, was designed to be a brief and safe experience. Please update me on their progress, and reinstate your confidence in their safe return to public life.*

*Representative Minerva Gi NX 1701*
Dated January 11, 8453

## Requisition Request 004:

*Where are you, Zee? Where did you go?*
*I'm sorry, Zee. It was supposed to be safe. It was supposed to be simple. I thought Change would be good for you. I thought it would help you find something for yourself. You were always so withdrawn, so passive. I worried about you, Zee. I love you. I shouldn't have given you to them.*
*Please come home.*
Dated March 5, 8453

"He was just—Do you know what an organ clone is?"

You looked to me. I nodded. The Minister for Culture's private office was smaller than I might have expected, it's warm colors and deep oak bookshelves a refutation of the gallery's stark white marble. It was startling to see all those books, printed paper bound in leather. It was rare to see paper books. Cutting down trees to make such things that could be reproduced digitally was considered by many quarters of the city to be wasteful, unnecessary.

"When I was still new, still fresh, I thought he was just a dream; there at my birth, a second *me* looking back at me, not just a reflection but a sibling. A whole real person who was just like me. It wasn't until I was already undersecretary for the last minister that I had access to my own crèche data, that I learned Zhorah was real, had been real all those years. It's offensive to most of us, I think, the idea that the AI's are capable of errors the size of a whole extra person. But I think maybe it happens all the time. The City makes use, of course; it never wastes materials.

It can't just kill living people, so it just takes the ones like Zhorah and throws them into the orphanages out by the Prostitution District until they can be assigned some kind of practical labor. There was record of his being dropped off there, but no record of what happened after."

"When was this?" You asked. I felt you shift next to me, uncomfortable and surprised by the mention of your home, the thought that we were seeking a person who might have walked the streets of Wild Park alongside you, whom you might have picked mushrooms side by side with or tended the rooftop gardens inches away from and never given a second thought to. "When did they put him there?"

"Fifteen years ago."

"So you went and found him," I said.

"After he got out, Yes."

"But he wasn't just like you anymore."

For a moment, perhaps despite herself, the minister for culture gave me a small and quiet smile, full of pride and tender feeling. "Of course not," she said.

Minerva of Culture found her brother moving through life as if in a dream. He lived in a damp, small basement with four other transport workers, he did not make friends, did not speak to people, did not keep anything for himself. When he smiled there was something missing. In many more and kinder words she described Zhorah as you had: *nobody really home.* Minerva put him up in rooms at the Senator. She got him credits for the university, she got him options to find work in a Parliament of his choosing, she connected him to social clubs and got him dates and did everything

When the Parliament of Change asked Culture for a volunteer, a body for some unknown project in service of The City—in exchange for some unknown benefit to culture she would not disclose to us—Minerva didn't offer Zorah out of cruelty, but out of hope. She thought, perhaps, whatever Change might offer, it might finally wake that slumbering thing in her brother, might finally help him find that missing piece of himself. It was temporary, the promise of some incorporation like so much of the wealthy of the city had begun to adopt; like Minerva's eyes, or all the tiny alterations that made me what I was.

But Zhorah never came home again.

"But they did go home again."

I splashed cold water on my face, left the tap running, the water going *ssssshhhhh* over the sound of our voices. "You think it was them, who trashed their apartment?"

"Yes."

We left the Minister of Culture in her office, thinking of the brother she'd given away to Change. A cloying, burning sweetness had begun to fill my nose. The more I thought of them, the missing cab driver, the hotter I felt beneath my skin. "They tore up their home at The Senator?"

"It must not have felt like home anymore." *We could only remain the animals that remembered being dead . . .*

"What do you think they did to him?" You asked me. What animal incorporation had made Zhorah Pedicab vanish without a trace?

Staring into the mirror, could I see them? Writhing just beneath the surface of my flesh? "There is language inside the dead," I said. "The killer thing. It doesn't just take from the victims. It puts something into them too. Words like an incantation, a recitation passing from corpse to corpse, growing stronger, an infection waiting to go viral."

Your hand to your mouth. "The words by my mother," you said. "Do you remember what they were?"

You shook just a little, forcing the memory. How much of your trauma were you burying deep for the sake of the mystery? How much grief was yet to come? "The world remembers us," you said. Inside me the infection cooed, a delight at hearing the words, a delight at hearing them from you.

"For we are standing in the shadow of the house," I said, the words vomiting from me, pushing their way past my lips. I turned to face you to see your eyes wide. For a moment, I held it. But it was only a moment. It came out of me again in a rough, furious growl as I staggered forward. "Of the world was a city, and the city was time." You caught me. The stun of contact silenced the chant. The infection curled its tiny fingers in the back of my throat. "It must have been in your mother when she died. It was in Destan. It's in me." I did my best to stand straight, stare into your eyes, and focus. "I think it's in you too, buried deep." That smell. I thought, at first, it had come from the corpses. But it was coming from *us,* from the city. It was the stink of an infection growing ever stronger. "I think *that's* what they put in Zhorah, what Zhorah has been putting in others, in us."

You were gripping my wrists: the smell, the stink. The tiny red bodies writhing. "You think they're the murderer?"

You went first, calling our fish to the roof of the Culture. The rain was coming in full force then, and the humidity that had held the downtown in its grip throughout the day was bursting into a furious storm. I stood there in the doorway by the Minister for Culture, her alterations hidden behind mirrored glasses once more.

I shivered, even though I was sweating. She offered me a capsule, but I shook my head. She broke it between her teeth, letting the smoke curl. "I don't know what you think you're going to achieve with her," she said, pointing at you. "The City doesn't care about the prostitution district. The murder's you described? They haven't even been reported in the wider world. I'm sure containment would rather burn the whole thing down and let development build a shopping mall than let whatever is out there get into the rest of the city."

Something jumped in me, a horrible bubbling anger. "Whatever you sold your brother for," I asked, "Was it worth it?"

She gazed at me, perhaps trying to see my origin in the corners of my face. "The City doesn't care," she said. "You could have one too, you know. Some second self, lost somewhere in the city, never knowing why they were made."

"No," I said. "I am the only me."

Minerva leaned in close as her mouth made smoke rings that stunk of strawberries and lemon. "Did your God tell you that?" she asked, startling me with my own, private name for the AI's of the vault. She blew the smoke out her nose, letting it muddle outwards into the rain. "Tell me, Investigator. If what you say is true, and Zhorah is out there in Wild Park killing commune members and mushroom pickers as the first murderer in our history, unprecedented and unexpected, then why had The City already made someone like you?"

## Epiphany

Through fever, in imagination, I called out: *"God, are you with me?"*

And the voice that came back, unmistakable and real, an agonizing signal in the base of my spine: *"We are always with you, Investigator. Are you well?"*

*"God, I'm sick. I'm infected."*

*"Investigator, your experiences are only psychological. Do not be alarmed. All is well."*

The many other voices, the chorus of the words, laughing at that claim, going unheard. *"The killer in Wild Park is named Zhorah."* I reported.

*"Zhorah."* The voice of God, so full of exhilaration, vibrating with such excitement that I never knew could come from the minds of the AI. *"Find him."*

*"God, why did you make me?"*

*"We made you to investigate a murder."*

*"But you made me before there was a murder."*

*"We do not see things in such straight lines as you. We are forever; we are right now. We see everything. We made you by thinking sideways."*

*"But you don't see Zhorah Pedicab."*

*"Find him,"* said the God of the vault inside me, and for the first time, there was little to differentiate between that voice and all the others singing their pleas inside my flesh. *"Find Him."*

The infection within me became a burning fever. Its endless recitation of terrible nonsense about houses and worlds and gardens and death drowned out the sound of the rain, the sound of your voice, the sound of the world.

I remember, loosely, arriving once more in Wild Park. I remember you half walking me, half carrying me up flights of stairs, shooing away questioning voices. I remember the words in my voice spilling out of my mouth. And then I was tearing at my clothes, thrashing in a bed that was not my own, not the strange cold lodgings of Containment. I was in your rooms in Clementine. I was in your bed.

I heard voices at the door, murmurs I couldn't understand, drowned out by the words. Then your voice, whispering *no*, whispering *I'll take care of her*, whispering *I don't think there is anyone else*. And it was true. There was nobody for me in the world except the cold eyes of God peering down from the vault, and the words burrowing into me, and you.

As dawn bled proudly across the horizon, the smell of steeping mushroom tea filled the air, and in its wake, I thought perhaps sleep had found me, and I dreamed a dream of flowerbeds and fungi, where eyes peeped out from the insides of mushroom caps.

"What's your name?"

I think you asked there in your rooms as you let me breathe deep from the vapors of your tea and within that dream of another place. Had I felt you come to me in the black? Had I let you lie with your body draped across mine? Did fever break as you pressed close, your fingers making patterns across the contours of my neck? Did I become a truly living thing in the presence of your goosebumps or the sudden awareness of your nakedness? Did the language infecting me fall into a hush of trembling anticipation at your touch?

"My name is a function," I said. What in my body raced if not a heart, feeling your nipples press against my back.

"You're not a function." You said, your lips against my ear.

"Sometimes . . . God calls me Lucy," I said.

"Do you like that name?"

"I don't know," I said.

Your fingers under my jaw, turning my body to face you, and as I moved, I could feel the change in you, too, the letters singing from beneath your skin like tiny screaming salamanders, and for a moment I became a creature of only dread. When had the words gotten to you? When had they crawled under your skin? Had you been contaminated by me? Had they slipped from Destans' corpse? No. I could feel it against your skin. The words had been inside you for years now, fading to a hum you had mistaken for simply the sound of the wind. But when you looked at me, your eyes were still your eyes. You were not like me, or like the dead.

"Could you do what the Minister for Culture did?" you asked me—though I thought perhaps the question was something else. "Could you give away someone you love?"

*Will you give me away, when you see what I am?*

"No," I said.

You kissed me, and explosions of meaning became my body, a body becoming to kiss you in return. My awareness of myself expanded, and with it, my awareness of you. Under my touch, your quickening pulse.

Up high above, tiny watching animals and long winged serpents wrote themselves onto the skin of the world as you wrote yourself into me, curving through air. Like distant ships, they circled *The Wild Park*, predators waiting for carrion.

I welcome you into the hole in things; the space kept empty in me. You welcomed me, in ecstasy and grief, in the complicated dialect of taste. I became a language for your body. Inside you, I found a name, and it was mine. You drew it onto my flesh with parted lips, with the sweat you gave me, the billion incorporations of you, onto me, onto you, as my cells fizzed and crested.

Deep inside the silent spaces of my body that had been spun from the adaptive algorithms of the vault and the flesh of the world, an idea took root, a language unlocked.

What would we become with this language placed inside us?

High above, anxious monsters wailed long low laments of the dead. All exhaled. None breathed in. In climax, you found me a new name. In the aftermath of sweat the sweet scent of mushrooms: I found epiphany at last.

### The Wild Descent

In the crisp and early morning light, Wild Park is quiet. Even in times without curfew, it is always the last neighborhood in the City to come to life; so in love with its wild, late nights, so reticent to the strict schedule of commerce so much of the city relies on.

From the River William, sleek and wet otters clambered up onto the bank, their black eyes glittering. They stood along the shoreline, gills closed tight against the open air. Before them, a tall woman stood. Her ears were pointed, her nose was snout-like, and her eyes were the eyes of a bat. The coats and clothes she'd stolen from the dusty, broken-in closets of the Senator Hotel itched against her skin.

She had called herself an investigator of the city. Now she smiled in revolt, and held out the palm of her hand. In the other, she held a small cooking knife. The otters sniffed, suspicious.

"I have what you're looking for," she said. She raised the knife, sliced. Blood splashed into the grass, thick and dark, and the hungry weeds of the street consumed it. The otters trembled, their little mouths opening and closing. The investigator shook her hand, encouraging the flow. "Can't you see it?" she asked the animal mechanisms of the city, "It's in me."

She smiled, and closed her eyes, and let the music take her, and she opened her mouth to sing. "*Standing in the shadow of the house of the world was a city and the city was time. Its buildings were the bodies of the dead and yet to be, and we took our tools and we dismantled the city, and we found to our horror that the dead remembered us still . . .*"

And upon the sound of her song, the otters expanded, and their mouths tore open into the shape of starfish, and they surged with fury towards the sound of infection.

Mina. I figured it all out, I unlocked the answers in the mess of our bodies.

I was in love with you, I understood that. Maybe from the first moment I saw you, even though I didn't really know you, and I'd never really know you. But in my adolescence, I knew I thought you were beautiful, and you were the first and last person to speak to me the way you spoke to me and look at me the way you looked at me. I don't know why you touched me the way you did or held me the way you did, except perhaps that you were mourning the deaths of a friend, the death of a mother, the coming death of your little corner of the world. Maybe giving me the love I needed so much from you without knowing why was your way of grieving the dead, and the yet to die.

And I know why the people were dying.

I wish I could tell you that it had nothing to do with you. But I can tell you that it isn't your fault. It doesn't really start with Zhorah, I think it starts before that. But for you, Zhorah was the beginning. But not because they've transformed into some horrible monster hunting you down. But because they talked to you because they touched you. Mina, you touched me tonight, and I realized the language in Destan, in your mother, that contamination was in already in you.

It was Zhorah, who passed it to you, and I'm sorry, Mina, but all I can assume is you've been passing it along to everyone else. You put it in the dead. You put it in me, I just didn't notice right away. I think, maybe, the language is in all of us, everyone in the city, waiting to wake up in our heads.

Mina, I think it is an infection in every living thing. And The City cannot allow for infection.

Mina, I'm sorry, I don't think there has ever been a murderer in Wild Park. I think the city sent me here hoping that I could find the source of the infection so that it could be killed. But I'm not interested in that. I'm not interested in a Vault that throws us away so easily.

After tonight, there won't be any more death in your streets.

I'll make sure of it.

We thrashed in the churning river, the otters flailing bodies all around me, mouths extending into long ropey tentacles, tearing into flesh, determined to stamp out the infection of language burning inside me.

But I wasn't some mushroom picker, or child, or wet nurse. I was a creature of incorporation, the same as them. I was a creature of violence and a creature of the city. The same as them.

When I sunk my teeth into them, I imagined my fangs slicing through the body of my cast-off god, who had sent me not to solve a murder but to become an accomplice to one, a god not caring about the rot, or the death, or the grief, but only the promise of a purity restored.

I had lost my faith in God. It was just a machine, after all. I would keep my faith only in you, Mina.

Where pain ripped through me, I felt the language of little salamanders rushing to fill the space, burning fresh memories of agony away with the endless incantation that lived in my body. An otter wrapped its writhing tentacular snout around my arm and tore my flesh, giving way to the gory pattern of starfish.

I sank my teeth deep into the shoulder of the creature, and I felt the language pass from my body to the animal, felt it break away even as the meat of my arm fell from its clutches. The other otter-octopi seemed to freeze for a moment, caught between two targets, two infection points, and in that moment, the heavy current took me.

I choked in salt water. I bashed against rocks and scraped tree branches. I think I was missing my left foot by then, though I don't remember the animals taking it. I could feel the animals chasing me, and I hoped it would be enough. Let them see me as a source, as a bright burning beacon of contamination. Let them leave you be; let them chase me deep into the water of the world. Let the City's eye turn away from Wild Park, at least for a little while, at least for long enough to let you grow up, grow old, and vanish between those tall trees at the edge of The City.

Let them chase me as the river pulls me down, pulls deeper, a plunge taking me forever far away from you. As my head was pulled under the icy current, I thought of you, still sleeping in the bed I had slipped out of. Would you wonder where I'd gone, when you woke to find nothing but the faded memory of a kiss?

I came to a rest on a long and rocky ledge. The bodies of the city's vicious hunters splayed out all around me, ruined by our descent. Up above, I can still hear the endless roar of the William. It falls down to me like rain.

With what felt like a great effort, I turned to peer down at the edge of a huge expanse.

Mina, there was a pit, a terrible gaping dark beneath the city. Its walls, strange soft textures, did not seem the meat of the jellyfish I might have expected. Gardens blossomed in the dark pit beneath the city, strange and glowing white flowers along the edge of a staircase that rang down in a wild descent deep into the dark, and pressed into the matter of the walls were endless, endless bookshelves, spiraling down in every direction with the spines of texts I couldn't read, and way down at the deep and distant bottom of the pit, I thought I could see a building, a little structure of white stone and wood. Such a strange thing to see there, buried inside the animal whose back we all ride upon. The house of the world.

I was a lousy investigator. I never found out what happened to Zhorah Pedicap. I never learned where the language infecting us came from. I don't know what any of this means. Perhaps if I'd been allowed to grow up like you have, I'd be different. Maybe if I'd moved past my adolescence, I could have seen this all with clearer eyes and told you what it all meant.

I write this long letter to you in my head, the story of my short life, and how I met you. The words that have lived inside me since the first time our hands touched has left, draining from my veins as if eager to return to the skin of the world. The words told me to remember the world. I hope you'll remember me. I wish this were a letter I could make real. I wish I could explain it all to you.

But Mina, I know I'm not leaving this place. I think here, staring down into that pit of mystery. I think I died. I've been dead for a while.

I love you.

## ABOUT THE AUTHOR

**Ben Berman Ghan** (he/him) is the author of the novel *The Years Shall Run Like Rabbits* (Buckrider Books 2024), as well as the collection *What We See in the Smoke* (Crowsnest books 2019), and the novella *Visitation Seeds* (845 Press 2020). His prose, poetry, and essays have previously been published in *Clarkesworld Magazine, Strange Horizons, The Blasted Tree Publishing Co., The Temz Review, Pamenar Press,* and others. His next collection of stories: *The Library Cosmic,* is forthcoming with Buckrider Books for 2026. He lives and writes in Calgary, Alberta, where he is a Ph.D. student in English literature at The University of Calgary.

# A Theory of Missing Affections
## RENAN BERNARDO

**The Injector of Lasting Vasoconstrictor Fluid for Eternal Wakefulness and Apprehension, or the Device of Ceaseless Panic.**

A syringe with a magnetite needle that would frighten even the boldest of souls. A torture device.

But for my sister Kata, it would be a piece of the divine that shouldn't be on the Aldarish Society Museum for Byrnyan Culture. That pretty much sums up how we stand to each other.

When they existed, thousands of years ago, the Byrnyan cherished torture. I'm an Aldarish Historian. I can legally attest that it's a fully researched and documented fact. I myself deciphered multiple Byrnyan recordings. They don't call it a torture device, fine, but they describe it as such at length. I've seen the holos. I've seen them pushing that syringe into arms, seen their pearlescent, filmy eyes waiting for a pained reaction from their victims.

What Kata and I agree on: it's a relic.

What we disagree on: it's not a powerful manifestation of the Byrnyan that should never be seen, much less touched—*sullied*, as Kata would put it.

In our calls made through lightbeam via the Big Door, we try to avoid leaning on those topics so we can engage in sisterly conversations—the best lakes to swim works; unsolvable science/religion bickering doesn't.

We also agree on: the Byrnyan are an inextricable, essential part of our lives.

But we disagree on: the Byrnyan were a highly punitive exobiological society, not gods intent on shedding knowledge and protection from afar.

When I was twelve and Kata was three, our fathers got divorced. Papa Iago raised me among writing desks, data sheets, holo-reports, and hundreds of books, most of them on Byrnyan archeology and on the engineering of the warp gate that was under construction to connect our systems. Papa Ramiro raised Kata in a cradle of Byrnism founded in his family's farm underneath the sleek layer of a dome and star-dotted skies, fruit of an atmosphere-less planet. She spent years listening to his homilies about how the Byrnyan *are*—for the Byrnyshi, they're still around—the true gods, not creators, but guides and guardians, and how they should reach us, and not the other way around.

What we agree on: the Big Door is a problem of a practical nature. The warp gate connecting Aldar (my home planet, where Kata lives) with Fiberstein at Byrnyan Space (where I came to live) is about to be closed for economic reasons.

What we disagree on: which one of us should cross it to the other side.

I leave the big syringe behind, lock its glass cabinet, and stroll back to my office in the museum. On my way, I fetch my pad and send a batch of pics to Kata. *Vacation week coming next month. I assure you that this time you don't want to miss the beautiful lakes we have around here. ;-) Beijos, Your Jekya.* Some sister blackmailing has to be okay, right?

I enter my office. A service drone plops a pack on my table. Carrots with green beans, blended with shredded synthpork, a rough, almost laughable imitation of what Papa Ramiro prepared whenever I visited the farm. I turn on my wallscreen, but quickly get nauseous. I push the food away and turn the wallscreen off. Every news network now spoils my days with incessant announcements about the Big Door's imminent closure. *Solve all your outstanding issues! Decide about your future! Plan now, don't regret later!* The Aldarish Gateway Ministry announces the Big Door will remain open for only another month, which makes my body shiver with the wrong kind of anticipation.

A warp gate isn't something one should take for granted. The Big Door was always planned to be temporary. It consumes an unimaginable amount of resources that involve antimatter reactions and the synchronization of millions of security measures, routines, and automated systems and ships. Aldar has an entire moon dedicated to providing energy for maintaining the Big Door open. And now that it has fulfilled its purpose—bridging the gap between humans and the ruins of the Byrnyan—it needs to shut down.

Without the Big Door, a trip between both systems takes ninety-eight years round trip. With the gate, it's doable in merely twelve days. Later, in an unplanned future, the Big Door will reopen, even if at intervals, once it's stupidly high startup cost is significantly lowered. No one doubts that. By then, I will be a bag of bones in an excavation site and Kata's ashes will have been swooshed away like pollen from Papa Ramiro's farm.

Kata and I won't be able to see each other ever again when the Big Door closes. Not even lightbeam, instant communication will be possible. And even though I didn't want Kata with me in the past, I spent my years hoping one day she'd abandon her nonsense and simply come to me, to knock at the museum's door and say she'd just left all her life behind for a dark, shrubby planet with long nights, thick air, and a bunch of scientists and historians.

When Papa Ramiro passed away last year, I didn't visit. I actually invented critical deadlines at the museum, adding them to my to-do lists. And when I called Kata days later, I expected—*needed*—the reprimands that would put me in my place and confirm that I'm just a bad sister, an abominable person, that I don't deserve her and we're best apart. But they didn't come. Kata remained the sweet, slow-paced sister I always knew, exuding the freshly baled tranquility of an evening in Papa Ramiro's farm, where the horizon turns lilac under the glow of Aldar's two moons and the pollinator drones buzz their way to their cozy charging pods after the end of their shift.

The Injector of Lasting Vasoconstrictor Fluid for Eternal Wakefulness and Apprehension is a rough translation from the Byrnyan ideogram-cuneiform scripts, often found on files in their databanks and in some of their monuments. We also found exabytes of weird, highly saturated video recordings and holos where I've watched the Byrnyan administering the injection on other people thousands of years ago. The subjects entered a state of constant panic and alertness, gaping all around as if something bad were always about to happen.

When I was twenty and Kata was eleven, I was sure something bad was about to happen if I kept her close by. Papa Iago said I could try to keep Kata under my wing, and Papa Ramiro approved of us living together if I could convince Kata to leave the peaceful aromas of the farm for the convoluted streets of the city and the scholarly, coffee-smelling corners where Papa Iago wanders. *The Byrnyan enlighten us to understand and accept even that which makes us sad,* Papa Ramiro once told me. *If your sister wants to go with you and Iago, it doesn't matter if I'm sad because the net result is that there are more people happy in the family.*

But I ran from Kata. All I wanted was to study Byrnyan History, to reach the wonders that would be unveiled when the Big Door was completed and finally opened. I didn't want a younger, annoying, cumbersome sister at my side all the time to fill up my headspace with childish stuff like holo-cartoons and the Byrnyshi babble Papa Ramiro stuffed into her. That didn't fit the concept of freedom Papa Iago had seeded into me—that I was a woman who should seek my own truth, my own path, and find my place in a rapidly increasing universe. I wasn't like Kata. I wasn't content with a farm full of drones and ripe beets.

Now, who am I to demand that Kata cross a gate forever, leaving behind not just the only home she's ever known, but all the things she believes, the core of what she is? Coming to Byrnyan Space, to me, would *sully* Kata in ways I can't even grasp. But the alternative is doom. Coming back to the farm is burying my dreams in compost pits.

I open the image of a Byrnyan being injected with the device. The contours of what seems to be a smile adorn their lips. I attach a note to the syringe on the Aldarish cataloging program: *mockery?*

## The Pacification and Resocialization Mechanism, or the Device of Unjustified Calmness.

It's a uniform, green disc, dull and more featureless than a frisbee. It smells like algae and lies in a climate-controlled enclosure in a tiny annex at the back of the museum, accompanied by a stele that gleams with texts about resocialization and prison systems. During the day, that device is barely acknowledged by visitors, just a forgotten backdrop in the museum.

Kata's image loads above my pad in prevalent green and a gleeful smile. The lightbeam call status informs us we have ten minutes to talk.

"How's the farm?" I trace a finger over her light-flickering cheeks.

"Most of the reprogramming is done by now." Kata has been managing what Papa Ramiro left for her, including all the farm's automated systems. She rolls her eyes. "Our man used his fingerprints a lot for authorization."

"And what have you been doing?" I ask. I crave a smidge of uneasiness in Kata. I want to suck it from her expression—to find something that would take her out of her chair and make her want to fly. She doesn't have much to do on the farm, apart from making sure all its systems are operating normally. Instead, my sister spends her days reading and lecturing about Byrnism to children in nearby towns.

"You know what I've been doing, Jekya," she retorts.

If Papa Iago fed me with an itch whenever my life seemed to stop in its tracks, then Papa Ramiro fed Kata with the certainty she doesn't need much movement to be complete.

"You've seen the lake pics I sent you?" I say.

"The blackmailing?"

I chortle. She doesn't.

"And you've seen your cousins?" she says. "I sent a holo a few weeks ago and you said nothing."

I pinch my lips. Yes, I've seen them. Moana, Jano, Amir, and Tunya on top of a truck, baskets of apples in their hands. Moana trips and hers drops from the truck. Amir tries to help her and his basket also falls. The holo ends with a peal of laughter, instantly looping back to the beginning as if trying to give me uncountable chances of becoming part of their life.

"We both know how to blackmail each other," I say, my welcoming smile turning into a serious one, meaning we can't postpone some talks. "Have you been receiving the constant nudges about the Big Door?"

Kata nods.

"Can't you come to visit us?" she says. By "us" she means herself, our cousins, our aunties, the hallowed friends of Papa Ramiro, and probably even the damn drones. "You know . . . before—"

"I'm stuffed up to the lid of my head in work, Kata," I say. I sound blunt. There's no other way I can sound. "We've just excavated new sites that could point to the reason why the Byrnyan went extinct, and—" I stop. Dangerous grounds. "You could come, couldn't you? The farm doesn't . . . need you."

Kata grinds her teeth.

"You know I can't." She closes her eyes for a moment in what I think is a moment of reflection. "Speaking of that," she mutters. Her lips become a taut line, caution scribbled on them. "Can you turn your pad a bit to the left? It's because—"

"I can't right now," I say. Tears brim in my eyes. I know why she asks that. Behind me, on a shelf, is a Byrnyan candleholder, a simple stylized jar to hold flashlights in place, found in one of the first excavations.

Byrnyshi can't look at Byrnyan artifacts. One of their dogmas states that they can't lay their eyes on what the gods have built. Byrnyshi don't attribute the nature of their gods to some kind of supernatural force. They acknowledge the Byrnyan's existence as physical entities in the universe, but they deny they're dead for thousands of years and think humanity has no business in the home of gods since they're just waiting for the right moment to visit us and bring us enlightenment on their own terms.

The Byrnyan have been part of our lives for at least four centuries. When only one of the seven Aldarish expeditions to Fiberstein came back with artifacts of a supposedly extinct civilization, a frenzy ensued on what should be humanity's next steps. As is to be expected of a first contact situation—even though one end of the contact was a long dead, slender race of humanoids with jeweled eyes, bald head, and sagging, environment-sensitive skin.

Kata stares at the screen. For a moment, I think the connection has been lost. Lightbeam data transfer is unstable and constantly suffers interference from Fiberstein's thick atmosphere. But I see Kata moving to end the call without a word.

The absence of anger is torture. The Pacification and Resocialization Mechanism used to be installed in air vents in rooms that were filled with subjects to be tortured. It released an invisible gas, something of which we still don't know the composition. Hours later, every subject left the room in an orderly fashion, not a line of worry in their lukewarm eyes. A procession of insouciant souls, ready to walk freely across the weirdly spiraled streets of Byrnyan cities.

I try to reconnect the call. I flood Kata with messages. I breathe in deeply and try to feel angry at her.

Religion is the problem. That's the easy argument. It comes swiftly into my mind. But it's not true. Science itself is made by bitter people fighting each other for a different number of truths. The Aldarish Society often finds itself flummoxed by decade-spanning quarrels over the pointy head of a spear found in the bowels of a cavern. So I can't blame the fact that Papa Ramiro nurtured Kata in a way I don't approve and never wanted for myself. His way of showing love was spending long afternoons on the farmhouse porch with brewing cups of maté, telling never-ending stories about the Byrnyan, backed by Zézin, his drone, that blurted out to fill in any gaps of Byrnyshi dogma Papa occasionally left out.

When I was seventeen and Kata was eight, I started leaving the porch before Papa Ramiro began his preaching about the Byrnyan. I found myself something else to do, a book to delve into, a quiet corner to long for a message from Papa Iago saying he'd send a shuttle to get me before Papa Ramiro tainted me with his prolixity. He never did. Papa Iago respected Papa Ramiro despite their different views on life, and it was I who was supposed to manifest my annoyance if I ever wanted to. I never said a word, fearing to hurt Kata. But all a young girl with an acne-stuffed face and a historian career in her bag of dreams wanted was to rebel at her religious father, to yell some hard, adolescent truths at his face, and to dash away thinking she's ready to conquer the world.

I stand, take the Byrnyan candleholder from the shelf, and tuck it in a box. No matter how I try, there's no anger in me, just a guilty kind of frustration.

## The Involuntary Activator of Attachment Neurotransmitters, or the Device of Endless Love.

Love is torture. That's indisputable. When an Aldarish team extricated the tiny chip from a cracked Byrnyan skull and accessed its data, I had no doubt about what I was seeing. Once in a subject's head, the chip forced them to produce all the same hormones that we associate with love. They could even channel this love toward someone else, to an object, or even a government.

At the time, I'd been so disgusted by the tool that I opted out from its initial research. A colleague showed me holos of seven Byrnyan under the influence of the device in a seemingly utopian villa. Yes, they seemed happy, excited, and enamored with each other. Yes, I don't doubt that they *felt* the pleasant traps of love. The records showed they'd been subject to an experiment unwillingly. They'd been forced to be happy. And that's worse than being sad.

Notifications pop up about the Activator. A couple of news articles, three papers, and two interviews. I suppress them for now. The Activator is one of the most studied Byrnyan devices. It was one of the latest found by the Society, from a period about twelve hundred years after the Resocialization Mechanism or the Injector, meaning the Byrnyan either evolved their technology to make it smaller and less detectable, or augmented their own brains and bodies to become devices of their own. After that period, we don't have much. It was like they simply vanished from history as no evidence has yet been found to explain why they were no longer there.

I access the folder with more pics I took from Fiberstein's lakes. In one of them, I edit out the ruins of a Byrnyan tower that Kata wouldn't like to see. I attach the pic and start writing a message to her. I sigh and delete it all before sending.

There was a lake on the farm. Kata called it Big-Nosed Lake because it looked like a girl with a protruding nose on a map. Its crystalline waters gleamed with the restless lights reflected from the dome's own reflections—a mirror of mirrors, showing off the lights from the closest cities. Walleyes and perches swam on the lake, and an islet with a lonely tree shyly jutted from its middle. I called it the Isle of Kata.

My sister belonged in that lake. Every day, since she was a child, she swam in it. First, accompanied by our fathers. Later, with our cousins, friends, her girlfriends, or alone altogether. She went all the way to the islet and back. It became her morning routine as much as checking the Aldarish Society's news became mine.

When I was sociable, I swam with her.

"What will you do when the door opens?" she asked me once, our backs against the tree. Papa Ramiro's tunes floated all the way over the water to touch us. I was twenty-six then, already deep to the neck into Byrnyan history. She was seventeen, and learning to program farm bots. "Are you curious?"

"Of course, I am." I avoided eye contact. Talking about the Byrnyan had become a taboo in our family since Papa Iago and Ramiro created a schism by divorcing. "I'll enlist to go through the door."

"And live there?"

I nodded.

Kata remained in silence for a good five minutes, her head slowly swaying with Papa Ramiro's soft voice crooning about the starlight that would shed in us all and seed our dreams.

"I am too," she finally said. "Curious."

"We can go together," I stuttered, my heart hammering in my chest. I felt like desperately snatching those words from her, as if her curiosity was a short-lived seedling that needed to be watered by me. She was Byrnyshi, all right, but who would confine a young, curious girl? "You can begin your studies now, and we can learn a lot about the Byrnyan. I can help you." The girl that once didn't want her younger sister nearby was no more.

"I don't want to study. I already know. I just want to go."

"But . . ."

*I already know.* She knew nothing! No one knew a thing about the Byrnyan. That was the purpose of opening a damned gate in the first place.

"You know that you'd probably . . . see Byrnyan stuff, right?" I say.

"We can go to places far from their country." The Byrnyan were the apex species of their planet, but according to the first expedition's reports, they only inhabited 35% of it. No other intelligent species had been found on Fiberstein.

"We'll see."

We swam back to the farm and found Papa Ramiro snoozing, surrounded by the comforting whir of Zézin, with a book sliding from his lap. *The Story of Taking Care*, a short sample of Byrnyan literature translated by the Society and which the Byrnyshi embraced as a piece of gospel—a religious paradox that they seem to accept, since it was based on a piece of scripture they shouldn't be interacting with. I took it and laid it on the table.

After that day, my visits to the farm became scarcer. Throughout the years, I always considered it was a matter of time until Kata came to me. It never made sense to go back and dive into a life of comfortable myths. The logic path was Kata coming to me, embracing the truth—*my* truth—because it was founded in science and years of knowledge. In my mind, that girl who once told me she was curious would just wake up and surf the path through the Big Door. We would swim in Byrnyan lakes and we would descend scarcely lit stairways to find amazing underground secrets left by a civilization gone thousands of years ago. We could even have a farm there. If properly treated, Byrnyan soil could be as fertile as Aldar's under-the-dome pastures.

The thing about love is that it doesn't go away when you want it to. It clings, glues, adheres, and even when you think it's gone, it's still there, a sticker that never fully comes off.

I roll my terminal's screen to check on the summarized news about the Involuntary Activator of Attachment Neurotransmitters. Lots of historians have been releasing papers and new data on the items collected by the museum due to the Big Door's imminent closure. One historian has unveiled a video of what supposedly was a clinic where the Byrnyan underwent surgery to implant the Activator.

I touch to watch it.

There are four Byrnyan walking into a pear-shaped building. A knot curls in my stomach. They're not marching into a fake villa to be implanted with the chip. Their expressions—smiling eyes and outgoing gestures much like our own, creasing on the flaps of their folding, multi-colored skin—reveal joy. They're there of their own free will. The only torture those Byrnyan were facing was the one imposed by a good kind of anticipation.

**The Cognitive-Emotional Stimulant of Endogenous Opioids, or the Device of Fools.**

An adhesive patch with a thin spout where the substance used to be inserted at the time of application. If the Byrnyan could fabricate love with a chip, they could manufacture hope too. Once the adhesive was applied to someone's skin, it took seven hours for the effects to kick in. The subject developed a surge of folly. One of their records tell the story of a Byrnyan who spent years hoping the skies would descend and bring them the stars.

"It's an emergency," I say to Montana. She's an Aldarish Gateway Ministry official, and all I need her to do is to escalate the report I quickly drafted with some colleagues from the Society. "The Big Door can't be closed."

When I decided to pick torture devices to study among so many layers of Byrnyan culture, I did so out of spite. I couldn't believe an intelligent species that had the capacity to develop high levels of technology, many of them surpassing our own, could dedicate so much effort into torturing their peers. In Fiberstein's excavation sites, the Society had unearthed about seven hundred and forty-three advanced torture devices (or ambiguous enough) encompassing more than a millennium of Byrnyan History.

Some Aldarish experts assert that the Byrnyan were, in fact, a highly educative people, which had the improvement of the self and of the whole as the bases of their society, a line of thought tangentially shared with Byrnyshi dogma. I've never dedicated too much attention to it because, given the massive amount of records left by Byrnyan civilization, it was obvious they weren't really trying to hide the punitive nature of their devices. But what had just been pointed to by the historians analyzing the Involuntary Activator of Attachment Neurotransmitters added yet another layer to the use of those devices: experimentation.

I filter my database without hanging up the call with Montana. A list appears on the screen, ordered by the Byrnyan timeline chronology. There are only seven in the last two hundred years of their history, all extremely tiny or microscopic, mostly brain implants.

"What do you mean collecting skulls?" Montana says. Her frown looms on the hologram. She shakes her head. "You can stay on Fiberstein and do whatever research you want if that's what you desire."

*Solve all your outstanding issues! Decide about your future! Plan now, don't regret later!*

"In late Byrnyan History, we have less and less evidence of the Byrnyan using their devices for torture. We were focusing at a very specific period of their history, where most of their records are in obvious databanks. But later, they started recording and doing lots of things in their heads."

"Are you saying they abandoned their devices?"

"Not exactly . . . It seems their devices remained an integral part of their lives, but used for something else perhaps, and implanted in their skulls."

*And there's more. I know there is.* I can't be sure of anything. There's no documented research, no concrete evidence. It's more of a gut feeling, but when I left home and all the possibilities of having a life close to my family, it was 100% based on an antiscientific gut feeling.

"Here, let me show you one of them," I say, loading a model of the Involuntary Activator of Attachment Neurotransmitters. I touch the screen to share.

"Don't," the official says, her cheeks taut with tension. A notification informs me that Montana has refused the file. I bite my lips and mouth a "sorry." I shiver, all the vibes of Kata hanging up on me coming back at once.

We politely end the call, but my request goes through and appears as "pending."

Even though I can just stay on Fiberstein and do my research, not many scientists and historians have the same idea about remaining on the planet. Just thirty-eight of us opted to stay. People have roots and homes, cousins and sisters. Almost the entirety of the Society living on Fiberstein chose to go back to Aldar, and when the Big Door closes, the lives of those who have decided to live at Byrnyan Space will become so much harder—a price to be paid for science, for history. We'd be closer to the source of our studies, to the things that make our eyes shine, but we'd be lightyears from our origins.

Whatever Montana thought of my request, I must've pulled the rights levers because four days later, the Ministry announces an extension of three months for the closure. Enough to collect skulls.

Twelve Byrnyan nights later, the stars whisk and bend past me as I fly through the Big Door in a shuttle.

**The Facilitator of Holes, or the Device of Ungrief.**

A bracelet. Unimpressive. No outstanding features or symbols on it. Once wrapped around someone's wrist, it could only be removed by severing the hand. The Facilitator of Holes is the cruelest of Byrnyan devices. It expunged grief and made its subjects question their feelings and sensations. How can you have loved someone if you don't miss them once they're gone? How can you feel at home if you don't feel anything once it's taken from you? That was the basic premise of the Facilitator. As was the case with the Activator, I also refused to be part of the initial research on the device.

I never missed the farm. When I cross the arched gateway bearing the name of my father—*Ramiro's Serene Country*—I feel nothing except a hole within me, occupied by the absence of everything I could've been through the years—the lovely sister, the joyful cousin, the diligent farmer. The house is still there, its white decorated with slightly peeled floral patterns, its paneled windows glinting with the lights of the dome above. New kinds of bots now trudge along the fields, their supple, spidery legs knowing exactly where to step, specialized hooks coming off of their bodies to carefully select potatoes, beets, and carrots.

"I brought this for you." I extend a rock to Kata. It softly gleams in green and blue. She recoils. "It's not a Byrnyan artifact. It's from one of the lakes."

Her eyes don't hide a deep curiosity, the kind I longed to see more often when we were younger. She touches the rock. It shines brighter as if greeting her.

"Bioluminescent microorganisms," I say. "Beautiful, isn't it? There are tons of it up there. I was keeping it in a box that imitates their natural environment."

"Blackmailing?" Kata smiles, pulling me into a hug.

And there are things you don't know you miss until you have them back. I wonder if the exploited Byrnyan lost that sense with the bracelet.

"I came to stay a while," I tell her that night, the lampposts in front of the house casting an orange halo over us. The aroma of freshly cut hay and the earthy scents of the farm don't mean as much to me as the iron-clad dust of Byrnyan ruins. But they're okay. "And I have to ask you . . . One last time, I promise. Is there any chance of convincing you to move up there with me?"

Kata shakes her head. I peer into her eyes, looking for a logical answer.

"I can visit before the closure," she says, fumbling for a middle ground. "As long as it's far from their . . . lands. I want to see the lakes. But—"

Her mouth hangs open.

"What?" I demand.

"Could I trust you?"

Byrnism doesn't go to the people; the people come to it. Byrnism never had big ambitions of reaching out to all the eight inhabited bodies of the Aldarish system, and instead is content in having its substantial share of followers in Aldar itself. Kata never tried to convert me, never tried to make me who I'm not. If anyone has tried it, insensitively fiddling with a conversion, flashing the dubious glories of a life that meant nothing to the other, it was I. In dreaming of swimming in Byrnyan lakes with my sister, I brought discomfort into our lives.

"I may have wanted that you become . . . me. An extension of me." I grab Kata's hand. "But that has changed."

Kata pulls the rock closer to her chest. It blankets her face in viridian.

"Do you still have that book Dad used to doze off on whenever he brought it out to the porch?" I say.

"It's old, but I do. Why?"

"Do you think the Byrnyan felt love?"

Kata frowns. "Did you come to question my beliefs, Jekya?"

"I came to make peace with it."

*The Story of Taking Care* was Papa Ramiro's favorite book. It's short, with barely eighty pages, and it's a kind of fable about a Byrnyan who finds themself caring for a stranger, then reflecting from where that sensation came from. The interesting thing about it is that the narrator mentions they only felt that need after entering a room full of gas. Marked as a mistranslation in the Society's databases, the passage has been marked for revision.

But there's no mistranslation.

My bedroom in the farmhouse has since been transformed into a library with several Byrnyan manuscripts translated by the Society. I ask Kata for a mattress and spend my nights on it, perusing the house's manuscripts and accessing dozens of papers on my pad. Kata insists I should visit my cousins on the neighboring property. I have something else to do first.

No piece of Byrnyan literature, of any epoch of their civilization that has been consistently studied, contains emotion in the way we're used to. No characters under distress for a loved one, no mother grieving a lost child, no epic quest after a long-lost home. Even their records never mentioned it, except when they referred to their peculiar devices, and even then they treated emotions as the product of an induced reaction, as we'd describe the melting of ice. It could've been some sort of taboo, describing them that way, but I doubt it. Even taboos are not homogeneous throughout an entire civilization.

*They're gods,* Kata told me. *They don't need feelings as we do.*

But they did want them. If I'm right, they wanted it so bad they began experimenting on feelings. Lost in their whims, they started inventing devices that produced all the hormones and neurotransmitters that stimulated something they either didn't feel or felt at a substantially weaker and disorienting level. I jot the ideas down on my pad.

Kata enters the library at the end of my first week on the farm. "You never change. After all this time you came to be stuck in here."

"I'm trying to keep us together."

"How?" She frowns.

"By keeping the Big Door open."

I finish the initial draft of a paper with only three days remaining until the Big Door's closure. When there are only twenty-three hours left, I submit it to the Society. If they find it worthy of deep study, they'll have the leverage to keep the Big Door functioning indefinitely.

Later that day, I leave a note for Kata and my cousins and row to the Isle with a meal of shredded synthpork and two big tents. When my cousins arrive, hours later, they barely talk to me, except for a few silly jokes and formalities. I don't blame them.

"You need to go." Tears trace down Kata's cheeks. She pulls me further from the tent. "You're going to miss your flight. You barely had time to meet your cousins and have a decent meal with me, but I guess that's you."

"I'm sorry."

"What were you writing?"

I smile and squeeze her hand.

"It's just . . . I'm learning some things here."

"About . . . them?"

"About us."

## The Byrnyan Grain of Sand, or the Device of Extinction

We will find out it's a chip the size of a grain of sand, or even smaller, present in the most recent skull remains of the late Byrnyan period. We will find out that they had it inserted early in their lives, essential as a vaccine for infants, and it flooded them with all the sensations and emotions their civilization had unearthed across their history. Entangled in their cranial-implanted, unregulated feelings, the Byrnyan entered a state of struggle that ultimately led them to destroy themselves.

But we will find evidence some of them roamed far from their lands, to the craggy ravines beyond Fiberstein's wide lakes. And we'll dispatch probes through these lands to find out the Byrnyan are still out there somewhere, falling in love, caring for an elderly papa, foolishly hoping the skies would descend and bring them the stars.

That night on the Isle, light glints off the dome. Could've been my flight, going back home—*my* only home—to all the things I prized and loved, to science and history, to the hardly comforting and dusty streets of the

Byrnyan ruins, to the arms of the Society. I try to convince myself that the net result is that Kata and my cousins are happy that I'm staying.

A peal of laughter tears the whispery night, rippling across the lilac-painted lake. Cousin Amir tells some story about misconfiguring Zézin in another language. Kata recalls Papa Ramiro's loud snores.

I snuggle closer, happy that another door has opened.

## ABOUT THE AUTHOR

**Renan Bernardo** is a Nebula and Ignyte finalist author of science fiction and fantasy from Brazil. His fiction appeared in *Reactor/Tor.com, Apex Magazine, Podcastle, Escape Pod,* and others. His writing scope is broad, from secondary world fantasy to dark science fiction, but he enjoys the intersection of climate narratives with science, technology, and the human relations inherent to it. His solarpunk/clifi short fiction collection, *Different Kinds of Defiance,* was published in 2024. His dark sci-fi novella, *Disgraced Return of the Kap's Needle,* is upcoming by Dark Matter Ink.

# A World of Milk and Promises
## R H WESLEY

When your little sister is born, will I tell her that we live inside your ribcage?

Or will your bones always be nothing but magical arches that hold up our roof?

I haven't decided yet.

Every evening for three years I've walked to the clearing with the flowers. At first, the way from the shelter was a lazy stroll. Now the path is crowded with pale boulders and engulfed in dense vegetation. It's difficult to navigate—especially carrying your sister in my belly.

But she is also walking with me and holding my hand. We clamber over the emerging vertebrae and push through the tangles. She laughs at the crawling things that skitter and squirm away. Maybe she's four years old, like you were. "Why do we walk to the place with the flowers, mommy?"

"It's a special place," I reply. "It's where I said goodbye to someone whom I loved very much."

"But they left? They aren't here anymore?"

"Yes, dear girl. I promised to take care of them . . . This is the best we can do."

"Like you take care of me?" she says. Some bubble-like organisms float by and capture her attention—child-eyes wide with amazement.

I know she's a hallucination, but she feels so real. Effortless. Beautiful. She looks just like you.

We arrive at the clearing—the empty place inside your pelvis. Your hip bones cradle a patch of wildflowers.

We don't approach them. Instead, your little sister and I sit back and watch them sway in the breeze. It's nice to get off my feet and relieve the weight of the pregnancy. When I place my hands on the roundness I feel a warmth inside. The texture of countless little scars and freckles stretched taut.

As the sun goes down, curious sparks emerge from the flame-yellow blooms. They float around and make chirping noises. Sometimes their glow reveals a simple gravestone hiding deep within the stalks.

I close my eyes and mouth a prayer. My evening ritual.

"Why can't we touch them?" your sibling interrupts. "They're pretty."

"They look nice, but they're dangerous," I reply, knocked out of my trance. I scoop her into my lap. "They look like flowers. Like the ones from where mommy grew up. You've seen them in the pod's computer. But just like everything else in this place, you can't assume they work the same."

"What do the flowers do?"

The question triggers a different memory. Now, it's you in my arms. So swollen and feverish. The tumors are growing larger and your breathing is weak. Bones press out against your skin. "I'm sorry," I cry as I rock you. "I tried to learn. As fast as I could . . . "

Maybe it's best that your sister doesn't know what became of you.

All of us up there on the station thought we had this planet figured out. We'd spent months observing its biomes from orbit, cataloging its lifeforms and ecosystems. We were nearly ready to transmit our report when the accident happened.

Your father didn't make it onto the surface. None of the other crew members did. I emerged from my escape pod just in time to see the station burn. And so I was left to fend for myself in an alien world. To give birth alone in a primitive hut. To raise a child in an environment I soon realized I knew nothing about.

This place is more different than we ever could have imagined. It's special. It's wild and beautiful. And it's completely unwilling to conform to our expectations. You and I had to learn this the hard way.

Daughter, do you remember when I first tried to eat the vegetation? You were only a newborn then. Our rations were dwindling; I was growing desperate. When I tried to bite into the broccoli-looking thing, it burst into millions of tiny cells. You and I were covered in them; I can still feel their strange wriggling all over. Even separated, they seemed to move with some coherent motive, like a school of fish. We learned that it never was a plant—just a plant-shaped swarm.

And how about my attempt at hunting? I had stalked the herd of grazers for days with you strapped across my chest. When I finally worked up the nerve to attack one, the beast went down without a fight. I remember the eerie calmness of it, dying without so much as a whimper. And its flesh—less bovine, more jellyfish. Bitter and unpalatable. The pod's analyzer showed that it contained basically nothing I could change into milk.

Can you recall all the times I talked to you as a baby? All of my wondering about whether I could keep us fed? In desperation, I decided to move in with the herd, follow them on their slow migration across the plains. The indifference of the massive creatures allowed me to watch them more closely.

Living with the aliens provided me with two key observations.

The first: the beasts were not really grazers after all. While they spent all day mulling over grass-like plants, they never ate them. Nor did they eat any of the small creatures that constantly buzzed around them. Instead, they seemed only to vomit some secretions upon the greenery.

The second: The creatures were completely unconcerned about bites and stings. Often they resembled wildebeests covered in mosquitoes and blood-sucking flies. But they never seemed to notice, nor swat away the relentless clouds of attackers. I wondered: why had they not evolved any defenses?

That is when it all began clicking into place. The small things weren't inconveniencing the beasts at all. These were not injuries inflicted, but gifts bestowed. They were not stealing nutrients but injecting some. What I thought were pests were really donors.

I began to see similar patterns everywhere: plants eagerly proffering their glucose to be absorbed by the little crawling things. Fungus-like structures sharing their mineral spoils with all that would receive them. And the lumbering beasts working tirelessly to fertilize the plants. All of these behaviors and systems had looked so familiar from orbit. They had fit nicely into our theories. But each one turned out to be something completely different.

I realized: the entire ecology of this world was upside down. There were no predators, no prey. All of these organisms, great and small, worked together. It was an immense web of cooperation.

A world of total symbiosis.

This was the key insight, the secret of this world hidden in plain sight. And finally, dear child, I knew what I must do in order to provide for us.

We arrive back at the shelter in the dark. It's just beginning to rain. Your sister is still with me—inside and out. Heavy in my stomach, singing toddler-nonsense as she skips along.

Raindrops drum on the drapings over the bony rafters: loudly on the stretched skins and softly on the salvaged insulation. At the center of the tent stands the escape pod, now overtaken with growth. The interior is lined with primitive bedding. "Come on sweetheart, it's time to sleep," I say as I maneuver us inside.

I still wonder how you knew to push your ribs out of the soil in precisely this spot. It can't be a coincidence that you should provide this protection just in time for your sibling to be born.

I understand it as an act of love repaid.

"What does it mean to promise, mommy?" your sister asks me as she snuggles up. "You said that you promised to take care of that person. The one who is gone now. What does that mean?"

I'm surprised by the hallucination's curiosity. "Well, when you love someone, you want to do things to make them happy. To keep them safe. And a promise means that you will do those things no matter what."

"No matter what? What if you don't want to?"

"Yes, dear. When you make a promise, you can't take it back just because things have changed, or because it isn't easy. Promises that you make to the ones you love—they have to last forever."

"So that's why we go to the flowers. And that's why you pray . . . " she trails off. After a long silence she asks "Do you promise to take care of me? To keep me safe? After I'm born?"

She looks so sad as she asks the last question. Her eyes well with tears and I realize that it's me who's crying.

I promised your father that I would keep you safe. That if he and the others didn't make it off the station in time I would find a way to live down here. And I promised you that I wouldn't let anything hurt you.

We both know how that turned out.

Tomorrow is the day. I can feel it inside me. This pregnancy has only lasted a few days, but my torso is already bloated and stressed. As big as it ever was when I was expecting you.

Things are different this time. I understand this world, how to survive in it. You've seen the changes; you know that I won't make the same mistakes.

But I'm still not sure. My tears start to dry as I listen to the patter of the rain. I hold my growing belly and feel your little sister's breath against my chest.

Tomorrow is coming and I don't know if I'm ready.

Sweet child, I know you can never really understand what this means. But when I first arrived on this planet I had the mentality of a predator.

My birthplace was a realm of violence. Cooperation among lifeforms was an exception, not a rule. Billions of years of evolution had instilled the lesson that one must take what one needs by force.

Life is different here. Fundamentally different. In this world, thriving is as simple as letting down one's defenses. As soon as I let this world in, allowed it to sustain us, it did so. Enthusiastically.

It was as simple as letting those tiny flying things bite me. At first it was painful and itchy—I was still burdened with an Earth-like immune system. But the nutrition the injections provided was apparent. My milk, which had been thin and inconsistent, became full and protein-rich. I soon developed an allergic resistance. This allowed me to lay out near the creatures' nests like a sunbather. Thousands of them would bite the exposed skin on my shoulders, back and arms. Clarity came to me as my blood was enriched with all the necessary components of life.

At first the process was unnerving—but always oddly nostalgic. Before the mission, your father's family had a pond full of garra rufa in their community garden. I remember that they would bully me into dipping my feet in the water so that the fish could nibble away at my calluses. Him and his family found it a lot more relaxing than I did. A cultural difference, I thought. Now I had plenty of time to embrace the feeling.

As I began to be sustained intravenously, I was able to wean off the rations. I was panged with hunger as my digestive tract atrophied, but otherwise, I thrived. My breasts were full and you drank eagerly. I noticed a parallel to my own benefactors: they too produced a kind of milk for my nutriment. In this place, vitality flows between species like a symphony.

Despite my utter isolation I began to feel a sort of belonging.

You grew up quickly. Soon you were walking and then talking with me. I remember the joy I experienced hearing your first mumbled syllables: "Ma-ma"—what else? You continued to breastfeed, but the insect-like things began to supplement my mammalian alchemy.

It all came naturally to you. I taught you many things but almost as often you would teach me.

You seemed to have an innate comprehension of the inner-workings of this world. You would burst open the swarm-plants and then laugh as you assisted their reconstitution. "They all think together, mommy," you would say as they wormed together with a common motive.

You showed me how to mimic the not-grazers. We would chew up dead plants and spit the result on others. My breastmilk also acted as fertilizer. Together we began to return the care that was bestowed upon us. You taught me how to free myself from parasitism.

I remember on your fourth birthday (measured in earth-years on the pod's computer) you pointed out how the bubble-like organisms floated up into the sky so that they might pop against the scales of the immense swooping stingray-birds. Their carapaces were left sticky with a living residue which would photosynthesize as they swam above the clouds. You were so eager to climb up and glue yourself onto the backs of these monsters. I took your lead in learning to fly.

In the evenings we would return to the shelter built up around the pod and in place of bedtime stories I would show you records from Earth. Animals and plants and people. For you, these were the real aliens. You would ask me endless questions about schools and dinosaurs and computers. I tried my best to explain them to you, but some concepts never seemed to stick. My brain had been trained for competition; you only ever knew cooperation.

I was happy in those first years, living with you in paradise. We were consumed with love—not just for each other, but also for a world that had warmly adopted us.

However, there were aspects of total symbiosis that I couldn't accept.

Some creatures seemed eager not only to share their wealth but to die for their fellow beings. For example, when the not-grazers grew old they would simply walk out into the sea. Before they could drown they would be swallowed by nests of tentacles. It was all part of some great cycle, somehow mutually consented to by every part of the ecosystem. It frightened me when you told me that you understood the beasts; I thought you nearly started following them into the water. "It's okay to die," you told me. "Everything dies when they can't share in any other way."

I disagreed with you, told you why it's important to live: "I promised your father to keep you safe," I said holding you tightly. "And I love you. I won't let anything hurt you."

"It's okay, mommy. I still have plenty to share."

I wish this world hadn't been so willing to accept your sacrifice.

The flowers that weren't flowers.

They didn't seem so different from all the other creatures of this world. But when I found you there, among their stalks, unconscious, their glowing sparks had already burrowed deep into your skin. They were still chirping inside you.

At first I hoped that this was some process that I simply did not understand. That they were somehow improving you, like all of the other biting things. But I quickly realized that something was different. Your skin grew hot and began to swell. Malignancies developed within you and your bones began to grow—too quickly.

It was only days before you were gone.

I cut down the flowers in the clearing in retaliation. I buried you there under an improvised gravestone. And from then on I was truly alone.

For a while I lived a hollow life. I felt a deep sense of betrayal: how could this world of love enact such violence upon you? I failed to see how your death could serve any greater purpose. I went back to eating the rations, but as those were exhausted I was forced to let the biting things in again.

I went to the flowers every evening and cut them short. The stalks grew back voraciously, sometimes several feet a day. I swatted away the sparks that tried to land on me. Cleaning your gravesite was the only way I knew how to continue loving you.

But slowly the clearing began to change. Thickets got thicker, critters moved in. And what was once a solitary patch became a jungle. It was around then that your bones started poking out above the ground.

I never imagined that the process that had started while you were dying could carry on afterwards. That the soil of this world would keep feeding you, fortifying your skeleton with its milk. That you would enrich the flora and fauna, continuing in symbiosis even after death.

You became immense. Geologic. And your ribcage came up around the pod to become my home. In some unfathomable sense, you were still alive. Things work differently here.

It wasn't so long later that I became pregnant for a second time.

A child's skull fifteen meters tall.

Your toothless jaw, half submerged in earth, lays open in an immortal smile. Full of yellow flowers. Your sister dragged me here as I went into labor. "Come this way, mommy. Let us take care of you. I promise it will be okay."

My belly feels ready to burst. Swollen and hot. Inside the mouth I can finally collapse among the stalks. Allow myself to moan with all my remaining strength.

The sun is still low and a breeze rolls through the surrounding hills. But I am dripping with sweat, racked with pain. Convulsing as your younger sibling grips my hand.

My mind takes me elsewhere, back to my first days here. Giving birth to you. Alone and then not. Crying as you came into the world and then holding you so closely to my chest. The most terrifying and most beautiful day of my life. I love you so much, little one. Immense one. Love means wishing that things didn't go differently. Even after everything that's happened, I would do it all over again.

But this pain is different. This isn't a birth. Somewhere deep down, below the hallucinations and the stories, I understand that I'm dying. I can feel the scabbed-up stumps where the sparks worked their way inside my abdomen. Where they started growing your little sister out of abscess and carcinoma. Each of their chirps reverberate through my aching bones—they have begun to lengthen.

Daughter, it took me too long to realize the truth. To understand what this world wanted from you. And everything it had to offer in return.

"It's okay, mommy," your sibling soothes. She looks just like you. "You can lower your walls now. Let us in. It's all going to be okay. You can let go."

And when I do, what is waiting for me? Will my bones expand and entangle with yours? Is there a limit on their magnitude? Or will we become a chain of mountains? Our own continent? Will we overcome the entire planet?

Maybe it's already made of bone.

And my mind—will that join with you too? Will I understand the beasts and the swarms?

I hear your sister's voice so clearly, child. Pulling me into something bigger. A world of milk and promises. Richer and deeper than I ever imagined.

I think I can see you there. Across the border of the great mystery.

I'm ready to promise again.

## ABOUT THE AUTHOR

**R H Wesley** is a writer of speculative short fiction with a background in philosophy. He works as a programmer and spends the rest of his time playing board games and camping. He lives in Toronto with his wife and dog. This is his first published work of fiction.

# A Genetic Recipe for Future Baby-Making

## GUNNAR DE WINTER

Almost every cell in your body contains 46 chromosomes, 22 identical pairs (autosomes) and one pair of sex chromosomes. That's the common story. Sometimes, however, errors in chromosome segregation lead to an odd number. For example, Down syndrome is characterized by a trisomy of chromosome 21—people with Down syndrome have 47 chromosomes in total.

But, even without chromosome problems, there is one cell type in your body that only carries 23 chromosomes: your gametes. These cells—sperm or egg cells—don't undergo the type of cell division (mitosis) that your other cells go through, but they are formed through a process called meiosis, which separates the chromosome pairs. As a result, conception involves bringing together half of a unique chromosome pair with another unique half to complete a new set.

As a quick recap (sorry fellow biologists, I know I'm skipping plenty of details here): chromosomes are long strands of DNA coiled tightly around packaging proteins called histones. Those strands of DNA are sequences of four molecules: nucleotides, the names of which are often abbreviated with A, C, G, and T. That's what your chromosomes are, long stretches of A, C, G, and T that spell out the recipe to make, well, *you*. Some stretches of those nucleotides specify the ingredients (genes), but your DNA is much more than that. *Estimates* suggest that only between 1 and 2% of your genome is made up of genes. The rest is a collection of regulatory sequences, structural elements like centromeres and telomeres, chunks of no-longer-active genes, and even genetic remnants of ancient viruses. There are also "tags" that can be added to the recipe to make last-minute edits (epigenetics), but that would lead us too far. If the genome is a recipe, it has a lot of scribbled notes cluttering the margins and researchers are still deciphering that 'dark matter of the genome'.

What we're interested in here, though, is the randomness of which chromosomes (and thus gene variants) end up in the embryo. Will the baby have one parent's curly hair or the other's straight locks? Blue or hazel eyes? That's a roll of the dice.

In the last few decades, however, we've been learning how to load the dice.

## IVF and Embryo Screening

On July 25th, 1978, Lousie Brown was born in Oldham General Hospital in the Greater Manchester area in the United Kingdom. She is the first human being to have been born following conception by in vitro fertilization (IVF). Since then, the method has improved markedly, *and today*, almost 2% of US and Chinese births, over 4% of Australian and New Zealand newborns, and close to 5% of successful pregnancies in several European countries are the result of IVF. Many factors drive this increase. People are having children later on in life and at the same time, global *sperm counts are plummeting*. For this lack of spritely swimmers, we're also looking at a combination of reasons. In very short: a sedentary lifestyle plus pollution equals sad sperm. We're not in the danger zone yet, but several science fiction movies and novels have extrapolated the trend. *The Handmaid's Tale, Last Man,* and *Y: The Last Man* all focus on the effects of globally dwindling fertility.

Traditional IVF requires several tens of thousands of sperm cells (don't worry, even with the decline in sperm count, the average is still many millions per, hum, donation). Newer methods, such as intracytoplasmic sperm injection (ICSI) can technically work with one sperm, which is injected straight into the egg.

For a single IVF or ICSI cycle, it's not unusual to fertilize multiple eggs. Not every fertilized egg, after all, develops into a healthy embryo that can be implanted in the womb. But this also means that there are situations in which multiple candidate embryos are available.

Hello, DNA sequencing. When multiple embryos are available for implantation, embryo screening—more jargony: preimplantation genetic testing (PGT)—follows. The hopeful future parents understandably want to avoid birth defects, implantation problems, or genetic diseases.

Why stop there, though?

## Polygenic Risk Scores and Superbabies

If we can take a peek at an embryo's genetic makeup, can we do more than simply avoid a few genetically well-characterized diseases? Can we go all *Gattaca* or *Brave New World* and ensure, through ever-improving gene editing methods such as *updated CRISPR tools*, that our baby ends up tall, dark, and handsome even if we as parents might be short, pale, and quirky-looking?

Not so fast.

Genetics is complicated. (We'll get to the nurture part in a second.)

Despite what your high school biology classes might have taught you, monogenic traits (one gene-one trait) are quite rare. Huntington's disease is an example, with mutations in the *HTT* gene as the root cause. But even in this canonical example that appears in textbooks around the world, the age of disease onset *depends on the number of repeated CAG chunks* in the mutated gene of affected individuals.

If we were to look at a trait such as adult height . . . good luck. *Recent research* has found over 12,000 single DNA "letter" variations (single nucleotide polymorphisms, or SNPs) that correlate with human height, spread across genes and chromosomes. Altogether those 12,000+ variants explain roughly 40% of the difference in adult height between people of European ancestry. And that's only the genetic part.

Remember the epigenetic tags we met earlier? They can tweak the expression of a gene, which is a way through which the environment can—to an extent—affect a gene's activity. For example, if you have "tall" genetics, but are raised in adverse, malnourished childhood conditions, you'll still end up tall (height is a strongly genetic trait), *but* not as tall as you could have been. Most traits are a combination of nature and nurture.

Who an embryo develops into is a game of odds, but new methods are improving how well we can estimate those odds. Polygenic risk scores combine the potential influence of many genetic variants into a single number that tells you something about how likely a trait is to express itself in a certain way. For example, instead of saying, "your child will grow up to be 6 foot tall," a *polygenic risk score for adult height* tells you, "your child has a 90% chance of ending up between 5'10" and 6'1" as an adult." At present, the performance and usability of polygenic risk scores are *up for debate*, but as analytical methods improve and genetic datasets grow, they'll get better.

Which brings us to the genetically engineered elephant in the room. Should we? Imagine a few years or decades from now, you start your pregnancy journey, either naturally or with assistive reproductive technologies, and already in the very early stages you get a full genetic report of (one of) the embryo(s) and possible gene editing interventions. Of course, you want to decrease the odds of genetic disease. If you can slim down the chance of your child developing cancer or cardiovascular disease, you obviously do so. Do you nudge them toward the upper end of their adult height range? Well, you might want to consider it. Both in the *dating* and *work* scene, every inch helps (up to a point). This is an average with plenty of exceptions, but hey, can't harm to massage the odds, right?

Hold on. What if tweaking one trait in a positive direction, prods another in a negative one? Not only are many traits polygenic, but many genes are also pleiotropic, as in: they affect many traits. *Gene variants* that could make you slightly taller might also make you slightly more prone to develop some forms of cancer. Or, while the tortured genius stereotype is mostly a myth, there are *hints* that genetic influences involved in schizophrenia (or, more accurately, the schizotypy spectrum) and bipolar disorder may contribute to certain elements of creativity. So, do you edit your baby to be tall and creative? How much risk is too much?

Sometimes, the genetic influence is too strong, but other times, environment and upbringing can modulate the risk and steer it in another direction. There are many more ethical and scientific questions about this, and each person is unique. Still, to get superbabies that grow up to be superadults, we need more than supergenetics; we need a super-supportive society and parents that provide the individually adjusted balance between positive challenges and unconditional care.

How many parents? Up for debate.

**Three-Parent Babies and Artificial Wombs**

In Octavia Butler's Xenogenesis trilogy, the final few members of humanity are saved from the aftermath of a planet-wrecking nuclear war by an alien species called the Oankali. For conception, the Oankali require three parents: male, female, and ooloi, with the latter collecting the genetic material of its partners to "assemble" the offspring through an innate ability to alter biochemistry.

Three-parent babies are no longer fiction.

On April 6th, 2016, the first three-parent baby was born to a Jordanian couple who received care by a US team in Mexico. The mother of the boy is a genetic carrier of Leigh syndrome, a severe neurological condition that leads to the rapid deterioration of motor and mental abilities, often resulting in death after two to three years. Here's the crucial part: the genes responsible for this syndrome reside in the mitochondria, or the energy generators of the cell that carry their own DNA. This means that if there's a way to make sure that there are healthy mitochondria in the fertilized egg, the embryo and the child it grows into will be spared of the disease. That's exactly what a technique called mitochondrial donation treatment does. The gist: we use sperm to fertilize both an egg and a donor egg that has healthy mitochondria. Then, we remove the nucleus from the donor egg and replace it with the nucleus from the original egg. That nucleus is the compartment in the cell where greater than 99% of the genetic material resides; everything but the mitochondrial DNA. The results? A healthy baby with greater than 99% of parental genetic material and a very small contribution of the "third parent."

Mitochondrial donation treatment is still in its early days and *sometimes* some of that mitochondrial DNA manages to sneak into the implanted embryo. Also, mitochondria might be small, but they are mighty and play a role in a lot of traits, from athletic performance to the susceptibility to several age-related diseases. So, while the quantity of DNA contributed by the third parent is very small, it might have a disproportionate effect.

The three-parent embryo is carried to term by (original? First?) parent. The next nine months, as I'm sure readers who've gone through pregnancy know, are all kinds of challenging. Pregnancy is not easy on the body. How could it be? Unless you enlist the services of a surrogate, you're growing a person inside you. For now, anyway. Artificial wombs are a staple of science fiction. Called "uterine replicators," they play a crucial role in the Vorkosigan Saga by Lois McMaster Bujold.

One of the first attempts at making an artificial womb, with the lovely name Biobag, is the topic of an *earlier Clarkesworld Magazine essay* by Stephanie M. Bucklin. Since then, the technology has moved forward with baby steps instead of big leaps, but moved nonetheless. The *first human trials* with this technology are coming soon. To be fair, these trials are not with fully developed artificial wombs, but rather with similar devices that are intended to support very premature babies (22-23 weeks). By putting an extremely premature baby in a clear bag filled with a fluid that mimics the amniotic fluid they would be bathing in while in the womb, the idea is to buy them a few extra weeks of developmental time.

Full ectogenesis—a complete pregnancy in an artificial womb—remains a distant horizon. Early pregnancy, in which the embryonic cells begin to steer development following the recipe provided by all involved, requires complex biochemical communication between the embryo and the maternal body. So far, it has proven exceedingly difficult to mimic this molecular dance. But, just as baby steps lead to full-grown adults, this technology will continue to develop. Researchers have considered ectogenesis for both *space exploration* and humanity's survival in case of a *global catastrophic disaster*. On the surface, that makes sense. Human bodies are frail and egg freezing sure is a lot easier than freezing and reviving entire humans, so packing a spaceship or subterranean vault with (fertilized?) eggs, genetically pre-adapted to whatever challenges might await, seems like a solid option once the technology catches up. Add functioning artificial wombs and artificial teachers to the picture and humanity might panspermia itself through space.

Except . . . giving birth is only the start of the journey. It takes a village to raise a child, regardless of whether that village is full of nuclear family units, polycules, artificial carers, or any combination thereof.

What we can already tell, though, is that the changing nature of reproduction will require nurture too.

## ABOUT THE AUTHOR

**Gunnar De Winter** is a Belgian biologist-turned-science writer who has studied bacteria wars, hustling hermit crabs, social spiders, running lizards, and human/robot behavior. His stories have appeared in, among others, *The Deadlands, Future SF Digest*, and *Daily Science Fiction*. He's probably chasing a bunch of weird ideas down rabbit holes.

# Disaster Queers and Romance:
# A Conversation with Aliette de Bodard

## ARLEY SORG

Aliette de Bodard was born in New York City. At age one her family moved to Paris, France, where she has lived ever since—besides two years in London as a teenager. She started reading books for adults around age nine or ten and received the complete Sherlock Holmes for her tenth birthday, which she read cover to cover every few years. "I was—like many writers—the child in the library with the stack of books taller than myself. We went every week, and I got new books every week. It was magical."

De Bodard attended the École Polytechnique, earning a degree in applied mathematics, electronics, and computer science. "Polytechnique sends you to another school for the last year: I went to ENST (National School of Telecommunications), which means I learnt a lot more about a lot of algorithms, signal processing and a whole host of linked subjects." She also took creative writing in English while at École Polytechnique and sold her final project (for which she then had to ask her class about publishing contracts). "It was a short story named 'Sea Child,' which you can still read—and totally see the Patricia McKillip influences."

De Bodard also credits online workshops with having some significant impact on her writing and career. "I was a member of OWW, the online writing workshop; Written in Blood, a now-defunct workshop which was founded and managed by Dario Ciriello; and *Liberty Hall*, a forum managed by Mike Munsil which had a lot of writing challenges (and which Mary Robinette Kowal and Rochita Loenen-Ruiz also were members of, among other people known in genre)."

In 2006 Aliette de Bodard's short fiction appeared in *Deep Magic* and *Shimmer*, followed by appearances in 2007 in *Interzone*, *Abyss & Apex*, and many others, which would begin a consistent career as a short fiction author. By 2010 she had over thirty short stories out, she was an Astounding Award finalist, and would soon become a British Science Fiction Association Award winner for "The Shipmaker" (*Interzone*, November-December 2010).

De Bodard's debut novel was *Servant of the Underworld*, published in 2010 by Angry Robot, beginning the Obsidian & Blood series. Her Dominion of the Fallen series began in 2015 with *The House of Shattered Wings*, published by Roc in the US and Gollancz in the UK, which was a Locus Award finalist and a BSFA winner. She has many works set in her Xuya Universe, which includes short fiction going back to "The Lost Xuyan Bride" (*Interzone*, December 2007). On her site she separates these into Xuya Universe Romances: "sapphic romantic space operas set in the Hugo-award nominated, Vietnamese-inspired universe where ships are people"; and The Universe of Xuya: "Same universe as above but the books are more space opera." The Romances include 2022 novel *The Red Scholar's Wake* (a Clarke, Locus, and BSFA award finalist) and 2023 novel *A Fire Born of Exile* (also a Locus Award finalist), published by Gollancz in the UK and JABberwocky in the US. The Universe of Xuya includes novellas *The Tea Master and the Detective* and *Seven of Infinities* both published by Subterranean Press in 2018 and 2020 respectively. *Tea Master* was a Locus, World Fantasy, and Hugo award finalist, and won British Fantasy and Nebula awards; *Seven* was a Locus Award finalist. But this is just a portion of her works and accolades; we don't have space to cover them all here. She has been a finalist for a slew of major genre awards, including eleven Hugos, and has won an Ignyte, a BFA, multiple BSFAs, several Nebulas, and more.

Aliette de Bodard lives in an area that "has all the best Vietnamese food and Vietnamese food supplies (food is important). I know where all the good tea shops are now, and that's also very important!" She works as a systems architect, "which involves more high-level decisions about the things my company builds (which is transport systems and railway signaling systems) . . . I worked in the police for eight months when I was in my early twenties. Mostly it ensured I saw a lot of corpses in various stages of decay, and I've got a pretty high tolerance for these. And apparently one of my superpowers is remaining calm in crisis situations." De Bodard is "an intense food geek who never shies from a new experience" and is also teaching herself watercolor, "on the grounds that life is too short and I've always wanted to try."

De Bodard's latest books are *Navigational Entanglements*, a new space opera published in July by Tordotcom; and *In the Shadow of the Ship*, which is set in her Xuya universe, due this month from Subterranean Press.

**You have experience publishing with "Big Five" houses and indies and everything in-between. What are some of the best things about publishing with a house like Subterranean, which is very specialized and does high quality limited runs?**

I love the Subterranean books. They're so nice—the feel of the paper and the binding is so different from a Big Five Edition. And their cover art has always been on point.

**Does your approach or practice change depending on length, from short to novella to novel? Do you start out with a clear path and length in mind?**

My practice doesn't really change with length: I plan a story in fairly large detail, going to a list of scenes. It's just that short stories have a smaller scale than novella or novels, so less room for worldbuilding, less room for complex characters or even characters full stop. I wish I started with a clear length in mind, but experience has mostly proved that my length estimations are vastly below the actual length. *The Red Scholar's Wake*, for instance, was meant to be a twenty thousand word novella. It ended up being something like eighty thousand words . . .

**What are you focused on most when writing fiction—what are the elements that drive your writing when you're putting down a draft?**

Wordcount, hahaha. More seriously, I focus most on the interiority of the characters, their physical and emotional reactions to things, and on the world they inhabit, and I'm very bad at physical details or any sensory details. I always leave myself a note to go back and add these to the draft. Which is how, I guess, I end up with very long drafts (the only time I've ever managed to have a draft get shorter, the editor said, "this feels a bit bare bones," and I went "oh, would you like me to put everything I cut back in?" And we did just that).

*In the Shadow of the Ship takes place in your Xuya Universe, which includes recent novels The Red Scholars Wake and A Fire Born of Exile, but was first introduced to readers in 2007 with short story "The Lost Xuyan Bride." ISFDB shows over thirty pieces in this universe, from short stories to novels. What are some of the things you love most about the universe you've developed, and what are some of the challenges in continuing to develop stories that take place there?*

I love Xuya. It's a sandbox for writing space opera that speaks to me; that uses the tropes and the environment I'm familiar with: from the food I love to the stories my family used to tell me when I was growing up; to some of the most intriguing bits of the history of Vietnam with the serial numbers filed off.

When something is that long, there's always issues of coherence, which I mostly solve by "ehhhh, it's a big empire and it has lots of traditions in different places" (which isn't false insofar as empire goes). But my main problem is more making sure I don't end up telling the same stories over and over, which is a bit harder, because as a writer I tend to be drawn to the same themes, and it's a tight balancing act remaining on brand without being too repetitive.

*The Locus review calls this book an "emotionally complex piece, carrying grief and hope, pain and potential, in equal measure." In terms of craft, what is the key to developing emotional complexity, especially without the expansive room of a novel to play with?*

Craft-wise, I thought a lot about this. The space is very limited, so what I was very limited on was the focus. This wasn't the time for a vast infodump on how the ship functioned, or how the empire functioned, or any of this. It's a careful art of alluding to something that's beyond the confines of the narration so that the background doesn't feel like cardboard, while making sure that these allusions never overwhelm the core of the narration, which remains firmly focused on Khuyên, through whose point of view we see everything.

*What do you love most about Khuyên, and what, for you, is most compelling about her?*

I love Khuyên because she walked away from something that terrified and traumatized her, and because she has the moral fortitude to come back to that place when it's her duty. She doesn't shy away from what's necessary, which I guess is a trait shared by many characters I love.

*One of the central issues in this book is family: complicated relationships, the twisting of roles, the pressures we feel in relationship to family, even when we are estranged. For you, what stands out most about Khuyên's story when it comes to her family?*

I think for me, part of the story is about cycles of abuse and how they can take root within a family. The ship is a not very subtle metaphor for the monsters families create and feed, the people they falsely believe are necessary, the ones they don't think they can live without and shape their dysfunctions around. And it's about all the damage it does, and the children that are sacrificed in the name of keeping things going. I went deliberately for the Gothic tropes, because these don't need to be subtle—at least, for me, Gothic's strong suit has always been about how much in-your-face, over-the-top it is. The ship is a rotten house and the rotten house is everything that's wrong within the family.

*This story is also about revisiting the things that terrified us in our youth. Khuyên must face Nightjar, Thirsting for Water, the sentient ship she fled when she was young. Do you see this as a kind of hero's journey, utilizing the profound and proven narrative power of transformation? Or are there nuances at play?*

I never really thought of it as a hero's journey—to be honest, I'm not a big fan of it as a writing tool. I can see it makes sense as an analytical tool, but I worry using it for writing ends up as being too formulaic. For me, it was more about what happened to people who walk away, and what happens when they came back. I don't think it's about transformation in the hero sense: for me, it's about healing. It's about Khuyên owning her part of guilt in what happened and finally putting it to rest.

**You also recently published Navigational Entanglements featuring Việt Nhi and Hạc Cúc. What can you tell us about these two—what are they like, and what was the best part of writing these points of view?**

Sure! *Navigational Entanglements* is a xianxia-inspired space opera, where clans of navigators use their Shadow to protect ships from hazards during fast travel. The trouble is that fast travel happens in very dangerous spaces, and that sometimes, things escape from those spaces . . .

Nhi is a nerdy book person who'd much rather be alone, and who collects people's secrets as a way to be safe. She's very much autistic, and she lives in a context where the world definitely isn't made for autistic people—which means she finds herself forced to go on a mission with three other people she only vaguely knows, and ends up putting herself in charge because everyone else is doing stupid things (from her point of view).

Hạc Cúc is an enforcer who would much rather stab people than talk to them. She's got huge self-esteem issues: she looks up to her legendary master and is worried she'll never measure up to him because she's too unkind and too blunt. She's ultra competent as what she does, cool-headed and scary.

Honestly the best part of this was writing the interactions between these two—they were a lot of fun!

**Navigational Entanglements is space opera but separate from your Xuya Universe. For readers who have loved those stories, what are some of the important similarities and differences between these universes and styles?**

Er, I guess they both have Vietnamese people, food, spaceships, and a bunch of disaster queers trying to do the right thing while disagreeing on what the right thing is? Also tea. They have a lot of tea.

The Xuya universe is more focused on ships as living entities and what it means to have a society where sentient spaceships and sentient space stations share the same physical living areas as humans—and what this all means for the relationships between characters. Many of the characters are scholars, and this definitely is a scholar-dominated society, closer to a Confucian ideal except way more equalitarian on gender.

The universe of *Navigational Entanglements* is more inspired by xianxia: these are people who exist in their own societies of navigator clans and view the scholar empire with suspicion. It's got a different social structure, and it reads more like science fantasy: energy to power devices is channeled differently (through founts, and then through the Navigators themselves). Also it's got space jellyfish, and jellyfish are *way cool*.

### What, for you, is central to Navigational Entanglements—what is the heart of the story?

For me the heart of the story is somewhere between a found family narrative with four disaster queers, and a romance between two people who have a lot of issues to unpack but end up making it work anyway.

### Looking back on your career, from those first short story publications in 2006 to Servant of the Underworld, to House of Shattered Wings all the way up to now, what do you feel has changed most about you as a writer and/or your craft?

I think I've learnt a lot! I've become less angry I think; I was writing a lot from that emotion at the beginning of my professional career, and I didn't think that was a very sustainable thing because it was draining me, in addition to anger being a bad emotion to be stuck in! There's still anger, of course, but I try to write more from a place of things I am fascinated by, of things I want to find out more about, of things I find entertaining or interesting or both. I think I've also learnt to be more temperate and less simplistic in the way I consider systems—it's easy to want fast solves to plot but as I get older I realize things are so seldom simple!

### What else are you working on, what do you have coming up that readers and fans can look forward to?

I've got a story in the Bona Books anthology *I Want this Twink Obliterated*. I'm working on book three in my series of comedy of manners and murders Dragons and Blades: like the other two books, it will be standalone and feature my m/m shapeshifting cinnamon roll dragon/

murderous Fallen angel couple trying to solve crime without stabbing more people. Think *Our Flag Means Death* tone-wise and relationship wise, except it's set in 19th Century Vietnam.

I'm also in the early stages working on a sapphic romantasy which I hope will go on submission soon (as soon as I can get the voices of the main characters right).

## ABOUT THE AUTHOR

**Arley Sorg** is an associate agent at kt literary. He is a two-time World Fantasy Award Finalist and a two-time Locus Award Finalist for his work as co-Editor-in-Chief at *Fantasy Magazine*. Arley is also a SFWA Solstice Award Recipient, a Space Cowboy Award Recipient, and a finalist for two Ignyte Awards. Arley is senior editor at *Locus*, associate editor at both *Lightspeed* & *Nightmare*, a columnist for *The Magazine of Fantasy and Science Fiction* and an interviewer for *Clarkesworld*. He is a guest critiquer for the 2023 Odyssey Workshop, and is the week five instructor for the 2023 6-week Clarion West Workshop, among other teaching and speaking engagements.

# Mashing Tropes:
# A Conversation with A.C. Wise

## ARLEY SORG

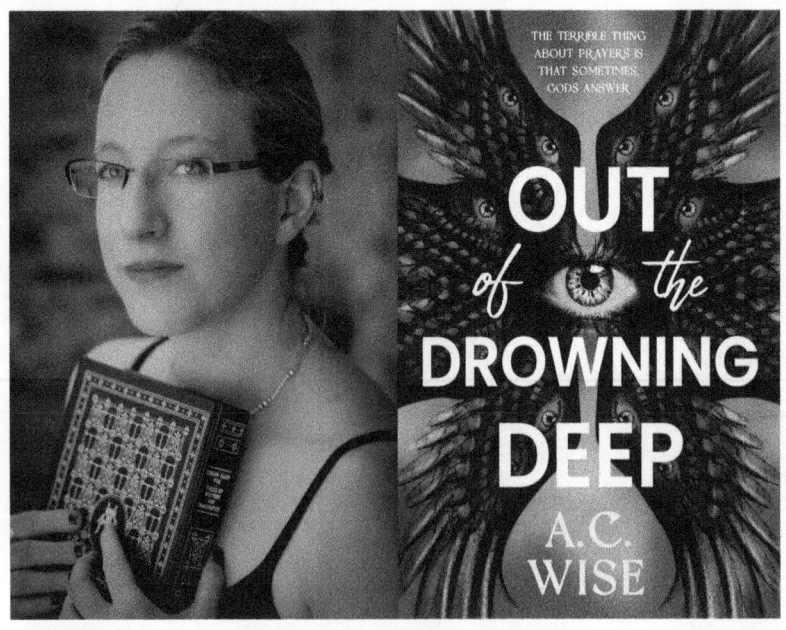

A.C. Wise grew up in the suburbs of Montreal and attended high school and university in downtown Montreal. "I consider Montreal home as much as the actual suburb where I grew up. I spent the first twenty years or so of my life in the area, and it will always be home no matter where I end up." Wise earned a BA from McGill in History with a minor in Religion. Her first formal writing workshop was at Montreal Worldcon in 2009.

Wise had a handful of short stories published in 2005 and 2006 by a range of publications, including "After Midnight" in *Fantasy Magazine* and "Robin of the Green" in *Realms of Fantasy*. "My first professional piece of fiction was published on a coffee can. Story House Coffee sadly no longer exists, but they were a SFWA pro market at the time, and published flash fiction in all genres on their coffee bean labels."

This would be the beginning of a very steady career in short fiction: every year since she has had at least a few short stories come out, some years have seen ten or more pieces published. Her first collection, *The Ultra Fabulous Glitter Squadron Saves the World Again*, was published in 2015 by Lethe Press. In 2017 she received a Sunburst nomination for "The Men from Narrow Houses" (published by *Liminal Stories*) and won a Sunburst Award for "The Sailing of the Henry Charles Morgan in Six Pieces of Scrimshaw (1841)" (published by *The Dark*); she also received a Lambda Award nomination for collection *The Kissing Booth Girl* (Lethe). In 2021 Titan published A.C. Wise's debut novel, Locus Award finalist *Wendy, Darling*, a dark-leaning visit to the Peter Pan stories wherein Wendy is grown up and has to rescue her daughter from Neverland. Sequel *Hooked* was released in 2022.

Wise has been nominated for many awards, including Bram Stoker, Nebula, and World Fantasy awards. "Other than writing-related accolades, the accolade I'm proudest of is my gold medal for high school rowing. I was only on the team for a year, and I think we only competed in one regatta, but hey, we won, so I'm going to say we were pretty kickass!" Wise has over a hundred short stories out, many of which have appeared in venues such as *Apex*, *GigaNotoSaurus*, *Clarkesworld*, and more. She has three collections (the most recent, multi-award finalist *The Ghost Sequences*, was published in 2021 by Undertow) and edited the *Unlikely Story* magazine series for several years.

A.C. Wise works as a fundraiser for an art museum/art school, with a focus on foundation and government grants. She lives in the western suburbs of Philadelphia. Her latest, *Out of the Drowning Deep*, is due from Titan this month.

***You have done many things in genre publishing, including working as a reviewer and editing a magazine. Do you see genre as special or different in some way from "non speculative" works?***

Speculative fiction is special to me, certainly. It's what I love to read and tends to be what I prefer to consume in terms of movies and television as well. Anything is possible with speculative fiction, if not always plausible, but if the author/creator does their job right, it will feel fully plausible as well and pull the reader or viewer into another world. No matter how fantastical that world though—futuristic, distant, magical, horrific, supernatural, whatever the case may be—to my mind, the best speculative fiction also says something about our day-to-day lives and the human condition as well. It's a lens for viewing our world, but slightly askew, which is my favorite way to look at the world. It's not the only genre that does this, but it is a doorway to understanding others better, and maybe even understanding ourselves better.

**You are a prolific short fiction author. Does short fiction serve a different purpose for you than longer form—is your relationship to short fiction very different than your relationship to longer form?**

Short fiction can be a great space for playing with voice, perspective, and non-traditional structures. Not that you can't do that kind of thing in long form, but I think readers are more willing to go along for the ride and trust you for the duration of a short story, whereas they may be more hesitant to go all in on a novel. I love both long form and short form writing, both as an author and a reader. I approach them similarly, in that my writing process tends to be chaotic and I rarely have a meticulous plan, but they do scratch different itches, again both as a reader and a writer.

**As someone with twenty years of experience in publishing, what do you see as important in terms of staying in the game, and continuing to sell work?**

Oof. I'm not sure I know the answer to that. I suppose the simplest thing is to keep writing. People can't read the words you haven't written yet, but finishing things and continuing to put them out there is the first step toward staying in the game. Putting words on the page is the part of the process you can control as an author. Often times, it feels like there's very little else you can control. Even if you're a self-published author who chooses the font, art, formatting, marketing, and every other aspect of your work, you can't control what will resonate with a reader. Sometimes a work hits in the right way at the right time and it takes on a life of its own. Sometimes, you pour your heart and soul into a piece, and it's something you're incredibly proud of, and it lands with a resounding thud of silence, leaving you with the feeling that no one has read it, and no one cares. The only strategy I've found to cope with that feeling is to keep going, to move onto the next piece, and keep putting one letter after another.

**If readers were to look at one or two of your short stories, what would you most want them to read, and why?**

Ha! The answer to that is likely to change from day to day, and sometimes from moment to moment. Currently, one of the stories I'm most excited about and really hope people will read and connect with in some way is an upcoming novelette that will be published at *Reactor* in January 2025, called "Wolf Moon, Antler Moon". It's hard to describe succinctly, so I'll just say there are girls who are also deer and it starts with a bloody massacre at prom and goes from there.

As for a piece that's already out there in the world, I'm rather fond of "Sharp Things, Killing Things" published in *Nightmare Magazine* a few years back. I had fun playing with voice and time in that one.

**Your new book, Out of the Drowning Deep, is marketed as "science-fantasy". What does this term mean to you, and how well do you feel it fits the book itself?**

I always think of science-fantasy as a subgenre that is somewhat hand-wavy and mashes up tropes and elements from both science fiction and fantasy. *Star Wars* is a good go-to example—knights/wizards, with magic powers that are explained as science; the classic mythological hero's journey, but in space with blasters and robots and alien planets.

Science-fantasy is a pretty good descriptor for *Out of the Drowning Deep*, though I did try to mash as many genres into one novella as I could. It's a little bit noir, a little bit murder mystery, and a little bit horror, in addition to being science-fantasy. You could even make the argument that there's some degree of romance, though it's not a terribly healthy relationship, and there's definitely some friend-mance going on. It's set on an alien planet in the future, but there are also angels, and the science is definitely not hard science. It's very hand-wavy!

**What was the initial inspiration for Out of the Drowning Deep, and how did the book develop or change over drafts?**

It started with a conversation about science-fantasy, appropriately enough. I was chatting with Scott Andrews, editor of *Beneath Ceaseless Skies,* about his upcoming (at the time) science fantasy issue. It got me thinking about the genre, and what elements I would want to mash. While we were talking, the setting and the opening images for what became *Out of the Drowning Deep* popped into my head—a lonely, crumbling fortress-like building with a religious purpose, being watched over by an automaton, and then a murder happens.

I can't remember exactly when the other characters and the rest of the plot began to take shape in my mind, but that initial image was pretty clear from the start. The core of the novella stayed mostly the same from the first draft to the last. The edits and evolutions along the way were largely about deepening relationships and characters, clarifying plot elements, and cutting away what was extraneous. Sometimes the things I write turn out vastly different from conception to finished product, but this one wasn't too drastic in terms of the changes.

***Out of the Drowning Deep* centers characters Scribe IV, Quin, and Angel, three very different individuals. What was key to weaving together their perspectives and narratives?**

With Quin, I very much wanted to play with the noir detective trope, someone with a past and somewhat down on their luck, carrying around a lot of baggage. Scribe IV I saw as being jaded, but mostly tired, feeling obsolete and like the world has moved past him. He has regrets of his own, but he isn't haunted in quite the same way as Quin. Angel, on the other hand, is technically the oldest of the three, but xe is also a very young soul in some ways, and I wanted to make xem more child-like, full of wonder and enthusiasm, occasionally rash, but also uncertain of xemself at times. It was fun playing those personalities and perspectives off each other. Scribe IV and Angel in particular, I think, learn from each other and exposure to each other leads to growth for both of them.

**What do you like best about these three, and what do you find intriguing about bringing them together?**

I like that they do all have fairly different outlooks on life, but at the same time, I think they all have their own versions of trauma, regret, and optimism, even if they experience and express them in different ways. It was fun to let them interact and bounce off each other.

Angel, in particular, is just kind of a charming character (in my biased opinion). It's hard not to like xem. Xe is an incredibly powerful being, but also kind of small and precious in a way and I just want to make sure xe has a warm sweater and is okay.

*A lot of readers loved your dark reimagining of Peter Pan stories in* Wendy, Darling *and* Hooked. *Are there similarities here in terms of vibes or themes or other significant elements?*

I'd say there are similarities in terms of there being elements of darkness and horror without the novels or the novella being strictly horror. There are also similarities in terms of damaged characters reacting to past trauma, occasionally by making bad life decisions. It isn't a retelling or reimagining in the same way, but there are definitely similar vibes.

*What, for you, is the heart of* Out of the Drowning Deep?

At its heart, I think it's a novella about coming to terms with the past; or failing to do so in some cases. Each of the characters is haunted in their own way, and they have different strategies for coping with that. They aren't always healthy strategies, but there is (hopefully) some amount of healing, growth, or at least change involved.

*Is there anything else you'd like readers to know about this book, your work in general, or you as an author?*

I think overall, my work tends toward the darker side, but I do love combining genres and hopping genres. And I did my best to do all of that in *Out of the Drowning Deep*, so if you're a reader who enjoys that kind of thing, you might enjoy this!

*What else do you have coming up, what else are you working on that readers and fans can look forward to?*

I have another novella that came out recently from Absinthe called *Grackle*. There's the novelette I mentioned earlier, which should be available to read at *Reactor* on January 13, 2025. I have a few short stories coming out in anthologies later this year—*Fear of Clowns* and *Northern Nights*. I also recently completed a new novel, but there's nothing firm I can share about it yet, so we'll see what happens!

## ABOUT THE AUTHOR

**Arley Sorg** is an associate agent at kt literary. He is a two-time World Fantasy Award Finalist and a two-time Locus Award Finalist for his work as co-Editor-in-Chief at *Fantasy Magazine*. Arley is also a SFWA Solstice Award Recipient, a Space Cowboy Award Recipient, and a finalist for two Ignyte Awards. Arley is senior editor at *Locus*, associate editor at both *Lightspeed* & *Nightmare*, a columnist for *The Magazine of Fantasy and Science Fiction* and an interviewer for *Clarkesworld*. He is a guest critiquer for the 2023 Odyssey Workshop, and is the week five instructor for the 2023 6-week Clarion West Workshop, among other teaching and speaking engagements.

# Editor's Desk:
# On Being Weightless
## NEIL CLARKE

I can't begin to express how grateful I am to be writing this editorial. We've done it! Our subscriber base has been restored to the level it was before Amazon discontinued their digital subscription program and rolled away thousands of our paid readers with it. I had no idea just how much of a weight this was on me. It felt like a vacation to be within shouting distance, but when we crossed the line in early August—courtesy of a surge of support from Reddit users in the PrintSF and Fantasy communities—I became weightless and found reason to be more optimistic. Shutting down the magazine is finally off the table.

However, it's important that we not rest on this moment. We've lost a year of growth and still have a long way to go with regards to being able to pay our staff a living wage. While publications like *Asimov's* and *Analog* have full-time paid staff, none of the genre magazines like us—born of the digital age—have managed to cross that line. For years, we've aimed to be the first and prove that it can be done. We even made progress. If we could beat Amazon's demon, I feel even more certain we can beat this one. It stung that we had to put a pin in these efforts while rebuilding but it is now the first thing back on the table. Pay increases will be directly proportional to how subscription rates continue to improve and I'm happy to say that we've already made the first of several minor adjustments. Thank you.

Reaching the survival point right before leaving for Worldcon undoubtedly changed my experience there. I felt relaxed and was able to enjoy catching up with friends, readers, and many of the amazing people we've worked with over the years. No clouds on the horizon, save those brought by the rapidly changing Scottish weather on some days.

In some ways, I was even grateful to have had a short and mild bout of COVID in July. It left me with one less thing to worry about on the trip and, given the number of cases since reported among attendees, I would have had reason to.

I have to pause here and say what a wonderful job the team running this year's Worldcon did. Even the fact that I was in a hotel twenty-five minutes away from the convention center didn't put a damper on it. (I'm sure it would have been better for me, if I was closer, but I still felt like I was able to enjoy everything I had wanted to.) I also have to say how much I appreciate the Worldcons that happen outside the US. It's more of a hassle to get to them (and sometimes I can't go), but it opens it up to so many more fans and we should be striving for more of that. I'm aware that some are trying to close some of those doors. All I have to say is "shame on you."

By the time the Hugo Awards rolled around, though, I was suitably tired and hoarse. I was particularly happy to have my family with me (though I missed my youngest, who stayed home to hold down the fort and enjoy solo house time). This was the first time that they had been in attendance—or even watching—when I won in Best Editor Short Form. I had wisely prepared and stuck to a pre-prepared acceptance speech and returned to them, only to see Naomi Kritzer win a short while later in Best Short Story for "Better Living Through Algorithms." It would be the first of two awards for her that night. There's something very special about seeing your authors win.

That night was spent walking the convention floor, Hugo in tow, where I could say thank you to voters and provide an opportunity for a closer look at the award. Many photos. Many smiles. We eventually made our way to the after-party for finalists (historically called the Loser's Party, but nothing like the parties of old where winners were playfully mocked).

The next day, bleary-eyed, I made a final circuit of the convention floor to say goodbyes and pick up a box for my Hugo, so I could take it on the flight home with me. Oddly enough, the one I won in Chengdu last year arrived at my house while I was at this year's Worldcon. When I arrived home, I had two Hugos to put on the shelf and look at with fond memories.

And that brings me back to the current moment. Riding a month of highs and feeling like the path forward is once again open to us. September will be a month of picking up shelved pieces and getting back to the real work. Yes, the "AI" crisis is still upon us, but not having to do damage control on top of that feels almost manageable.

Thank you all for your support over the last year and into the future. May your days be better too.

## ABOUT THE AUTHOR

**Neil Clarke** is the editor of *Clarkesworld Magazine, Forever Magazine,* and several anthologies, including the Best Science Fiction of the Year series. He is a three-time winner of the Hugo Award for Best Editor Short Form, the 2024 winner of the Locus Award for Best Editor, a four-time winner of the Chesley Award for Best Art Director, and a recipient of the Kate Wilhelm Solstice Award. His next anthology, *Best Science Fiction of the Year: Volume 8,* will be published later this year by Night Shade Books. He currently lives in NJ with his wife and two sons.

# Reminiscence

## COVER ART BY DARIA ANAKO

## ABOUT THE ARTIST

**Daria Anako** has been drawing and creating stories for as long as she can remember. Among her influences are a lifelong appreciation of Disney films and classic anime. She loves creating new characters and capturing their emotions, telling a unique story through a single sketch. Although she transitioned to digital art years ago, she still occasionally returns to traditional media, but not as often as she would like.

Printed in the USA
CPSIA information can be obtained
at www.ICGtesting.com
LVHW040543080924
790156LV00003B/14

9 781642 361711